*Colt shifted his partially clad body
closer to Kati and reached
for the baby.*

"You have to be tired of rubbing his back.
Let me." A delicious fluttering began in Kati's
stomach at the sight of Colt's strong hands, large
and dark against the small baby's blue fleece
bunny pajamas. The picture was beautiful, moving.
She had to look away.

The baby sighed deeply, his little arms and legs
going limp as Colt's hands worked a magic
rhythm.

"I think you've got the touch," she said.

"Yeah?" Colt looked pleased. "I never thought he
liked me."

Kati grinned. Who wouldn't like Colt Garrett? "I
think he's finally comfortable enough to sleep."

Very gently he lifted the baby and stood cradling
the child in one arm while he extended the other
to Kati. She knew touching him was a mistake,
but she just couldn't help herself. Taking his hand,
she let him pull her up until she was no more than
a breath away from his naked chest. Moonlight
gilded them, the cowboy, the sleeping baby and
the nanny.

The nanny, she had to remind herself. She was
only…the nanny.

Dear Reader,

The summer after my thirteenth birthday, I read my older sister's dog-eared copy of *Wolf and the Dove* by Kathleen E. Woodiwiss and I was hooked. Thousands of romance novels later—I won't say how many years—I'll gladly confess that I'm a romance freak! That's why I am so delighted to become the associate senior editor for the Silhouette Romance line. My goal, as the new manager of Silhouette's longest-running line, is to bring you brand-new, heartwarming love stories every month. As you read each one, I hope you'll share the magic and experience love as it was meant to be.

For instance, if you love reading about rugged cowboys and the feisty heroines who melt their hearts, be sure not to miss Judy Christenberry's *Beauty & the Beastly Rancher* (#1678), the latest title in her FROM THE CIRCLE K series. And share a laugh with the always-entertaining Terry Essig in *Distracting Dad* (#1679).

In the next THE TEXAS BROTHERHOOD title by Patricia Thayer, *Jared's Texas Homecoming* (#1680), a drifter's life changes for good when he offers to marry his nephew's mother. And a secretary's dream comes true when her boss, who has amnesia, thinks they're married, in Judith McWilliams's *Did You Say...Wife?* (#1681).

Don't miss the savvy nanny who moves in on a single dad, in *Married in a Month* (#1682) by Linda Goodnight, or the doctor who learns his ex's little secret, in *Dad Today, Groom Tomorrow* (#1683) by Holly Jacobs.

Enjoy!

Mavis C. Allen
Associate Senior Editor, Silhouette Romance

Please address questions and book requests to:
Silhouette Reader Service
U.S.: 3010 Walden Ave., P.O. Box 1325, Buffalo, NY 14269
Canadian: P.O. Box 609, Fort Erie, Ont. L2A 5X3

Married in
a Month

LINDA
GOODNIGHT

SILHOUETTE *Romance*®
Published by Silhouette Books
America's Publisher of Contemporary Romance

To the men in my life:

Dwayne: Gentle soul whose love runs deeper than words.
Mike: Who keeps me close to God.
Travis: "Beloved son in whom I am well pleased."
Cody: Truly a gift from Heaven. Thank you for the joy you are.
Gene: God in his kindness and wisdom knew how much I needed you.
Thank you for loving me.

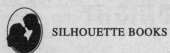 **SILHOUETTE BOOKS**

ISBN 0-373-19682-2

MARRIED IN A MONTH

Copyright © 2003 by Linda Goodnight

Visit Silhouette at www.eHarlequin.com

Printed in U.S.A.

Books by Linda Goodnight

Silhouette Romance

For Her Child... #1569
Married in a Month #1682

LINDA GOODNIGHT

A romantic at heart, Linda Goodnight believes in the traditional values of family and home. Writing books enables her to share her certainty that, with faith and perseverance, love can last forever and happy endings really are possible.

A native of Oklahoma, Linda lives in the country with her husband, Gene, and Mugsy, and adorably obnoxious rat terrier. She and Gene have a blended family of six grown children. An elementary school teacher, she is also a licensed nurse. When time permits, Linda loves to read, watch football and rodeo and indulge in chocolate. She also enjoys taking long, calorie-burning walks in the nearby woods. Readers can write to her at linda@lindagoodnight.com

All underlined places are fictitious.

Chapter One

Kati Winslow took a deep breath, exhaling with a shaky sigh. The next few minutes could mean the beginning—or the end—of her dreams. Perched on the edge of a heavy leather armchair in the very masculine office of the Garret Ranch, her palms grew damp just thinking about this crazy plan of hers.

The next few minutes could mean the end of *her* if she didn't handle things right. Any man wild enough to throw his leg over the back of a Brahma bull was certainly capable of tossing an impertinent woman out the same door she'd come in.

But she'd face a wild bull rider or even a mountain lion if she had to. Anything for Kati's Angels.

Checking one last time to be certain her imagination hadn't run away with her again—that she really and truly had an appointment with Colt Garret—she glanced at the newspaper ad crumpled in her lap like a hamburger wrapper.

"Cowboy has motherless baby. Urgently needs live-in child care at Garret Ranch."

The ad was followed by a phone number, a list of qualifications, and the words *exceptional pay.*

All well and good, but it wasn't the job she needed. It was the man who'd placed the ad—former rodeo cowboy and present owner of one of the biggest spreads in north Texas—Colt Garret.

Kati's heart did three back flips and a full Gaynor at the thought of the man who held her future in his hands, a man who'd held a special place in her heart for more than ten years. A man who didn't even know she existed.

Nervously she brushed at the skirt of her only decent suit, flicking away an imaginary speck of lint. Kati hoped the mint-green skirt and matching jacket looked mature and sensible. More than anything she had to convince Colt that she was not as crazy as she was going to sound.

She swallowed the dry lump in her throat and, for the hundredth time, rechecked her appearance. Sensible white heels flat on the floor. Skirt carefully pulled over her slender knees. Pristine white blouse buttoned to the top. The entire rig was so totally out of character, if Colt didn't hurry up the neat knot of hair would become a waterfall of dark, straight locks hanging down her back. And she'd be forced to kick off these pinching heels.

Where was he? Her gaze flicked anxiously from the fancy cowboy art hanging over the fireplace to the acres of lush green pasture visible outside the picture window and back to the solid oak entry. During their phone conversation, Colt had stressed his desperate need for a nanny. Under the circumstances that was exactly what she wanted to hear. But if the situation was all that urgent why hadn't Colt met her at the door instead of that tattooed man who looked as though he'd stuck his finger in a light socket? And where was Colt now?

She twisted her foot, feeling the first warning twinge of a toe cramp. Just as she bent for a foot massage the study door flew open and a harried looking cowboy, cradling a screaming, flailing baby, charged into the room. Kati straightened suddenly, the cramp forgotten in a rush of emotion.

Even unshaved and rumpled, Colt was more gorgeous than she remembered. Her heart joined her toe in a vicious cramp.

Wide-shouldered, skinny-hipped, he wore a red Western shirt that accentuated his darkness. Faded Wrangler jeans followed the angle of long, muscled thighs. Above a pair of red-rimmed eyes the color of Hershey's Kisses, his dark brown hair needed a trim.

He was tall and trim and gorgeous, and he stopped dead in his tracks at the sight of her.

"Are you Kati Winslow?" he asked above the din of the wailing infant.

So he didn't remember her. That much, at least, was good. If he had any idea she'd once fancied herself in love with him, he'd never fall for this scheme.

"Yes." She struggled to meet his gaze, worried that her too-wide eyes would betray the terror gnawing at her insides.

"Let me see your résumé."

Willing her hand not to tremble, she gave him the paper and was surprised when he handed her the baby in return. While he examined the sheet, she sat down again, laid the fussy infant over her shoulder and gently patted his back. He was soft and warm and clean but squirming miserably. Within seconds, he burped loudly, heaved a shuddering sigh of relief, and snuggled into her neck, his little head lolling to one side in exhaustion.

Colt looked up, expression stunned. "You're hired."

"What?"

He nodded toward the baby. "He's stopped crying. That's good enough for me. You're hired. Can you start right now?"

Kati batted her eyes, confused. "Right this minute?"

"I'm desperate." Wearily he collapsed into a high-backed chair behind the desk and slumped forward, resting his arms on the polished top.

She hoped he was as desperate as she was.

Kati considered his bloodshot eyes and bent posture. His exhaustion was so complete that she actually felt sorry for him. But she couldn't let her sympathy get in the way. For once in her life, she had to think ruthlessly.

"May I ask where the baby's mother is?"

Colt scraped a hand over his whiskers. Out of his mind with exhaustion and, if he was willing to admit it, downright terror, he hardly knew where to begin. How had this happened to him, a die-hard bachelor without a paternal bone in his body? How had he come into possession of a three-month-old child?

"It's a very long story, but if you're willing to listen…" Colt glanced up. Through blurry eyes he saw her nod, so he plunged in, reliving the fateful day three weeks earlier when he'd opened his doors to insanity.

Within ten minutes after the nervous little messenger had appeared at his door, Colt had run the gamut of emotions from disbelief to pure terror. Pacing the length of his ranch-style living room, he'd stopped now and then to stare from the blue-wrapped bundle in the stranger's arms to the papers in his own hands. His mind reeled with what he'd read there. Some woman he'd never heard of had sent him a baby to care for.

"How could anybody leave an infant in my custody? I don't know anything about kids." Colt shook the paper beneath the other man's nose. "Just who is this Natosha Parker, anyway? I've never even heard of her."

The messenger broke out in a sweat and hugged the door handle a little harder. Colt paused long enough to catch his breath, and the poor hapless man took that as an opportunity to escape before the big cowboy really lost it. He eased the door open, clearly hoping to Hannah that the wild-eyed rancher didn't yank him backward through the keyhole.

"Beats me, sir," he said, backing out the door. "All they told me to do was bring the baby out here to one Colt Garret." He shoved the infant into Colt's arms. "That's you, and I'm outa here."

He whirled and bounded across the concrete porch.

"Wait a minute," Colt yelled at the retreating form. "*Who* told you to bring the baby out here?"

The messenger didn't wait around to answer. He crammed the ordinary-looking brown sedan into gear and hightailed it down the long driveway toward the gate, fishtailing beneath the Garret Ranch sign.

The baby, whose tiny form was strapped into a carrier of some type, chose that moment to awaken. A high-pitched wail rent the country quiet. Cole pivoted from the front window where a rising plume of dust was all that remained of the retreating sedan. He shoved a work-hardened hand through his hair, sending thick, brown waves in a dozen different directions, and stalked toward the hallway.

"Cookie, get in here," he bellowed. At the sound of

shouting, the baby jerked, his little arms flew straight up and he wailed all the louder.

Cookie, chief cook and general housekeeper for the Garret Ranch, scuttled in from the kitchen. Twigs of hair stuck out on his head like blackjack sprouts. A battleship tattoo, a result of one wild weekend in Hong Kong, sailed his arm from shoulder to wrist. A white chef's apron covered the forty extra pounds of paunch around his middle. He was a scary sight, but the bachelor brothers of Garret Ranch didn't care. He made a mean chicken-fried steak, and that was really all that mattered.

"What in blue blazes is all the racket in here, boss?" His voice, a startling replica of an air horn, made the baby cry even more.

"It's a baby."

"A what?" Cookie backed away.

The sight brought a momentary, though not too happy, smile to Colt's face. "I said a baby, Cookie, not a rattlesnake."

"Same blame thing. Only, I know what to do with a rattlesnake." He shuffled over to the couch and peered down at the screaming infant. "Whose is it?"

"For the time being, he's mine."

Cookie plopped down on the couch beside the crying infant and began to laugh. The sound rumbled like a passing train. "One of them lady friends of yours finally got you, didn't she? You gave her a baby, and she gave him back to you. I knew it. I knew it. I told you that wild living would come home to roost some day, and it sure enough did. Here it is in the flesh."

Cole was dumbstruck. "You think this is *my* baby?"

"Ain't it?"

"No!"

"You sure?"

Of course he was sure. He hadn't done any "wild living" in years. Well, months, maybe. And the few times he'd been with someone he'd been very, very careful. He and his brother Jett had long ago made a pact to remain footloose and fancy-free. They were cowboys who loved their freedom and their wide-open spaces. No women or kids could tie them down. No sirree, not the Garret brothers.

The baby's cries had turned to shrieks. The tiny face was a wrinkled, purple mess.

"Do something, Cookie."

"Me?" The older man shook his head, setting the blackjack sprouts aquiver. "It's your baby."

"What do you suppose he wants?" Side by side, the men stared down at the infant.

Cookie, who thought food was the answer to every problem, hit upon the perfect solution. "Maybe it's hungry. You suppose there's a bottle or something in one of them bags?"

Colt hadn't even noticed the three bags leaning against the wall just inside the front door. He hurried to them, searching for something—anything—to make this little fella hush up. An array of plastic diapers, blankets and tiny clothes were stuffed into the bags. One by one he threw them out, scattering baby items all over the thick, brown carpet.

"Aha!" he cried. Delirious with relief, he withdrew a filled baby bottle and carried it back to the couch. The baby lay in his padded carrier thrashing his arms and squirming like the rattlesnake Cookie had likened him to. Colt pushed the bottle into the infant's open mouth. Instantly the baby quieted.

"Just like feeding a motherless calf," Cookie commented as the child latched on to the nipple and sucked greedily.

"This is a lot more serious than a calf, Cookie. Babies need attention all the time, not just morning and evening. We've got to find this baby's mama and send him home."

"Cute little feller, ain't he?" Cookie stroked one fat finger along the baby's cheek. The child turned his head toward the finger, a pair of brown eyes searching Cookie's face. "How could any mama worth her salt dump him on a stranger's doorstep like this?"

"According to the letter, the mother doesn't consider me a stranger. That's the odd part of all this. I don't remember ever meeting any Natosha Parker, but this paper says I'm the only person she trusts to take good care of little Evan." He looked up and grinned. "I guess his name is Evan."

"Don't make no sense, boss. If you don't know her, how can she trust you?"

"I don't know." Thoughtfully Colt rubbed at his whiskers. "Maybe I should call the sheriff and turn the baby over to him."

"And have him wind up in one of them homes somewhere? We can't do that to this little feller."

Never one to shun responsibility, Colt knew Cookie was right. The papers looked legal and in order, granting him complete and total custody of Evan Lane Parker, two-month-old son of Natosha Parker. He'd handled enough of his own stock contracts to know airtight legal work when he saw it.

"That's the answer, Cookie." He slapped the papers against his knee. Once more the baby jerked his hands into the air. "These are legal papers. Some lawyer drew them up for this Natosha Parker woman. I'll call Jace

Bristow and have him take a look. He can trace the mother through these papers.''

Jace Bristow had been Colt's attorney since the two graduated from Texas A & M. He was a great attorney and an even better friend. If anyone could trace this baby's mother, Jace could do it. Colt breathed a tentative sigh of relief.

Cookie, however, looked doubtful. ''What do we do with him in the meantime?''

Colt hunkered down beside the couch, his eyes on the baby. The little critter didn't look half so scary with his mouth closed. Fact of the business, he was downright cute sucking on that bottle with such heartrending desperation. He wasn't bald like most babies Colt had seen. He had a smooth cap of dark hair above a round face, a tiny bit of a nose and a pair of big brown eyes that followed every move Colt made. Someone had lovingly dressed him in blue overalls, a soft red shirt and a floppy cotton sailor hat that had fallen off during his fit of crying.

Who are you, little man? And where did you come from? Colt wondered, as he stroked a finger over the velvety soft hand. Evan responded by wrapping his own tiny fingers around the much larger one. At the unexpected rush of emotion, Colt gently withdrew his hand and straightened. He was a responsible man, a decent man, but he was not daddy material. Never would be. He sure as blazes couldn't go getting attached to somebody else's baby. And he had a real bad feeling that would be mighty easy to do.

''I've got a ranch to run. You'll have to look out for him.''

''I didn't hire on to take care of no babies,'' Cookie

protested. "I feel sorry for the little feller, but I'll quit if you try to turn me into a nursemaid."

"Come on, Cookie, you spent twenty years in the navy. Surely, you can handle a baby for a few days."

"Weren't no babies in the navy. I got my hands full cooking and cleaning for you and that bunch of ranch hands. I ain't doin' it. You'll have to hire a baby-sitter."

Suddenly an unpleasant odor emanated from the couch. Colt wrinkled his nose and looked from Cookie to the straining, red-faced infant. Cookie roared like a mad bull and beat a fast retreat to the kitchen. Totally defeated, Colt stared after his cook and then down at the gurgling baby. That was the moment he knew that his life would never be the same.

"So," he said wearily to the prospective nanny, motioning to the baby in her arms. "That's all I know about Evan's mother."

He didn't bother to tell her the rest. That live-in help was next to impossible to find because of the ranch's isolated location in the middle of miles and miles of cattle range. Nor did he mention his less-than-stellar bachelor reputation. No use telling Miss Kati Winslow all that, or she'd up and run out the door and leave him with this unhappy baby.

"Trouble is, I don't know what I'm doing and he senses it. He cries all the time. Never sleeps." Colt's shoulders sagged. "I think he hates me."

With each word, Kati's foolish heart lifted a few inches. He really was desperate. She just might be able to pull this off. "Have you considered turning him over to Social Services?"

Colt wagged his shaggy head. "Even though there are some good foster parents out there, I just couldn't bring myself to do it. For some reason Evan's mother trusted me to care for him, and I'm going to do that until I find her."

Sadness shimmied through Kati, her thoughts centered on the poor abandoned baby in her arms. This little boy had narrowly missed placement in foster care, a life that Kati knew all too well. She'd do anything—anything to spare him that. Her desire to care for him shot up a notch. Certain she was helping all concerned, Kati buried her nose in Evan's soft, powder-scented neck and battled the guilt of using Colt's kindness against him.

"I'm sorry, Mr. Garret." With steely determination she stood and tenderly handed him the sleeping baby. A puzzled Colt slipped his dark, powerful hands beneath the child, cradling the small body against his wide masculine chest. Kati glanced away and gulped. In the next two minutes she needed to be convincing, not moved to tears by the sight of a big ol' cowboy holding an innocent baby.

Drawing upon a lifetime of pretending, Kati took a deep breath and coolly announced, "I've changed my mind. I'm not interested in the job."

Colt looked stunned. Panic filled his bloodshot eyes. "What? No. You can't do this. I need you. He needs you." He came around the desk holding Evan against his shoulder with one hand while extending the other in a pleading gesture. "Please. The salary is good. You'll have your own room, your own cook, the run of the place."

She shook her head. "I apologize for the inconvenience, but the baby's mother could return at any time. There's no job security. Furthermore, the ranch is so secluded."

Colt's dark-brown eyes locked with her gray ones,

using every ounce of his persuasive charm. If she hadn't fully intended to take the job—under her own terms, of course—she'd have buckled from the pressure. The look Colt gave her was enough to melt the polar ice cap. And Kati was a marshmallow.

"Please," he pleaded hoarsely, "I'll pay you whatever you ask. Anything at all."

He moved nearer, bringing with him the scent of man and baby mingled pleasantly together.

"You're the only qualified applicant I've had." He sounded pathetic—and smelled wonderful. "The references you gave me over the phone all checked out. I'll raise the pay. Heck, I'll even…buy you a car. You *have* to take the job."

He stood within a breath of her, staring down into her face with such earnest persuasion that Kati was on the verge of agreeing to anything he asked. She tried backing away before she lost control of the entire situation. Colt reached out and touched her arm. Like the time all those years ago the thrill of his touch rendered her senseless. She couldn't think. Her head started chanting Colt's name.

"Anything, Kati," Colt begged. "Name it, and it's yours."

She was mesmerized. A moth over the flame. A deer in the headlights.

"Anything at all," he said softly, seductively.

Her heart thundered. Her ears rang. She couldn't think straight. Why had she come here, anyway? Oh, yes. Because of Colt. To marry Colt. That was it.

"Marry me," she blurted.

He stared at her as though she'd grown horns. She wondered if she had. This wasn't the way she'd planned to say it. She'd wanted to remain rational and logical while they hammered out a business deal. Instead she'd become the blathering idiot of her nightmares.

Slowly, Colt withdrew his hand and took one step backward. His horrified gaze remained riveted on her face.

As her good sense returned, Kati squirmed beneath his appraisal, equally as horrified. This was her one chance. If she blew it now, there would never be a Kati's Angels Child Care.

Having already crossed the line, she straightened her shoulders and plunged in. With every bit of enthusiasm, logic and rationale she could muster while shaking in her shoes, Kati tried to convince him that the plan was simple, easy, and helpful to all concerned. The bankers of Rattlesnake wouldn't loan her the money to build a child-care center unless she had collateral.

Collateral? What a laugh! To build her dream child-care facility she'd have to borrow the money for everything from the land to the building and even for the first few payments until the center began to turn a profit. And she could only think of one way for a single, jobless orphan to acquire that much collateral. According to the bankers of Rattlesnake, a husband's collateral would be just fine. But did she have a husband? Not even a boyfriend. And then she'd seen Colt's ad, and like a gift from heaven the idea came to her.

"So, if you'll marry me," she concluded, "I'll have the collateral I need to get a loan, the children of Rattlesnake will have someone to love and care for them, and you'll have a nanny, free of charge, for Evan until his mother returns."

In the course of her monologue, Colt's horror had turned first to bewilderment and then to incredulity.

"Even if this idea of yours made any sense at all—

which it doesn't—it wouldn't work.'' Colt gave his head a stubborn shake. "I don't want to get married. Never have, never will. Marriage sucks all the life out of people.''

"I'm not talking about a real marriage.'' She hoped she sounded calmer than she felt. "It's a business arrangement, a marriage in name only as a means to acquire collateral for my loan.''

He shook his head, jostling the bundle in his arms. "Your reasoning makes no sense.''

"It does to me. A fifty-fifty proposition. You get a nanny. I get collateral.'' Couldn't he understand? As long as they made a deal in which each party benefited, she was a businesswoman, not a charity case. She'd had enough of that in her life.

Shoulders sagging wearily, Colt pressed a thumb and forefinger into his eye sockets. Little Evan's whimper brought the big cowboy's head upright. Panic filled his dark eyes.

"Just a business arrangement, right?'' He patted the baby's wiggling back in awkward desperation. "None of that till-death-do-us-part stuff?''

"Of course not. After I have my loan and Evan's mother is found, you can go somewhere for one of those quickie divorces. No strings attached.'' While her belly shook in trepidation, she spoke lightly, airily, as if she proposed a marriage of convenience to a strange man every day of the week.

Surely he could see the logic in her win-win idea. He needed her almost as much as she needed him. As tired as he was, he couldn't hold up much longer. He was about to fall over now. And so was she. If Colt didn't say something soon, Kati would collapse in a heap on the scuffed toes of his black boots.

Still eyeing her with deep suspicion, Colt rubbed at the back of his neck. "Quickie divorce? Where do they do that?"

Kati blinked, uncertain. "I— Reno maybe?" She didn't have a clue.

"I don't know, either. My attorney would know."

Her pulse rate shot up. He was weakening.

He blew out a long, gusty sigh. "Would you be willing to sign papers agreeing to everything? The divorce and all, I mean?"

She really wanted to feel sorry for him, but she couldn't allow it. For once in her life, she had to be utterly, completely ruthless. Kati's Angels depended upon it. This precious little boy depended upon it. And the lonely, neglected children of Rattlesnake depended upon it—and her. The vision of Kati Winslow, guardian angel of needy children, bloomed in her imagination.

"Certainly I'll sign papers. This is a business arrangement." Nerves rattling like marbles in a tin can, she offered one last piece of bait. "I'll also sign a prenuptial agreement to the effect that I have no right to any of your financial assets."

"You're nuts, you know that?"

Gripping the smooth back of the leather sofa, she willed herself to hang in there. She could do this. She had to. This was her one and only chance to fulfill the dream of a lifetime.

"I am not crazy. Just desperate like you. Each of us needs something from the other. This is the perfect solution."

His lips twisted wryly. "*Perfect* isn't the word I'd use to describe it."

She shrugged, hoping for nonchalance. "Well, perhaps you can find some other nanny for the child."

Gathering her purse, she battled her conscience and looked toward the door as if to leave.

The baby's whimper grew louder.

"No!" Colt shouted. His hand snaked out and snagged her arm. Colt thrust the fussing child toward her. "Please. Three weeks is all I can take. You're the only human being that's agreed to accept the job under any circumstances."

Carefully extracting her arm from his strong, warm grip, Kati stepped back, refusing to take the baby. It wasn't an easy thing to do considering how much the baby needed her, and how pathetically Colt begged, but he was almost hers. She couldn't fold now. "Well, then?"

"I can't just up and marry a woman I don't know. What if I don't like the job you do with Evan?" His gaze fell to the fidgeting baby in his arms. "What if you're a lousy baby-sitter?"

"We aren't called baby-sitters anymore. We're nannies."

"Will you consider a trial run?"

"What exactly do you mean by that?"

"Move in with us for a few weeks until we see how things go. If your work is satisfactory and Evan is still with me, I'll—" He seemed to strangle on the words.

"Marry me?"

"Yeah. That."

"Will you sign a paper to that effect?"

In spite of himself, Colt grinned. She'd used his own words against him. She might be nuttier than a pecan pie, but she was smart. Not as smart as he was, though. He'd had plenty of experience dodging wedding bells.

He only needed her for a few weeks tops. By then, Natosha Parker would be found, and Miss Kati Winslow would be out on her conniving little—ear. Meanwhile, he could resume his work and get a decent night's rest. Evan would have the good, motherly care he deserved instead of the fumbling efforts of an exhausted cowboy and an old sailor. The little nutcase was right. She had the perfect solution.

"Yes, I'll sign the blasted paper."

He handed her the baby again, and this time she took him, hardly able to believe she'd actually pulled it off as Colt strode to the desk and began scribbling on a sheet of paper.

Reaction set in. Legs trembling so that she could barely stand, Kati settled back on the couch and hid her face in the baby's neck. She'd done it. Colt Garret was going to marry her, and she'd finally have children to love and a place to call her own.

The infant made soft, mewling sounds in her ear, a reminder of the most important part of the deal. Pressing him into her shoulder, she patted and rocked until he settled once more into slumber. He was so helpless and innocent that an enormous wave of protectiveness surged through her.

I'm sorry, baby, that I had to use you this way. I'll do right by you. I promise.

"Here you go, Miss Kati," Colt drawled, handing her the agreement. "I, Colt R. Garret, do promise to marry you one month from today in the event that Evan Parker is still in my custody. How's that?"

"Everything seems in order." Taking care not to wake Evan, she folded the paper and slipped it inside her purse. "A month should give us plenty of time to plan an appropriate wedding."

Colt thought his head would explode. "Now, wait a minute, here. I never agreed to a wedding."

"This paper in my purse says you did."

"It says marry, not wedding." Suddenly he was having second thoughts. If she started planning a wedding, half the county would know about it, a most disagreeable situation that would make shaking her off all the harder. Besides, he didn't really plan to marry her. That was just a ploy to make her stay with Evan.

He pressed down on his head with both hands. What had he gotten himself into? Didn't he realize he was too exhausted to make sensible decisions? Hadn't he seen that on television? Men do stupid things when they've been without sleep for days on end. Bright, sensible men became blundering idiots when sleep deprived.

He'd known this woman was a loony toon when she'd first started talking about marriage. Now she was demanding an "appropriate" wedding—whatever in the Sam Hill that meant.

Kati shot him a look of exasperation. "You can't get married without a wedding."

"Yes, we can. Couples do it all the time. I know a justice of the peace down at the courthouse who can marry us in two minutes flat." He snapped his fingers. "Just like that. In, out. No fuss, no bother."

Kati shifted the baby to her other shoulder. When he fussed she patted absently at his back, a natural motherly gesture that caused Colt's stomach to lift the way it did when his truck took a hill too fast. He averted his eyes and tried to concentrate. Lord only knew what he'd fall into if he didn't pay close attention to Kati Winslow.

Colt flopped down on the opposite end of the long leather couch and scrubbed his eyes with the heels of his hands. Lord, he was tired. "This isn't going to be a real marriage."

"We've already determined that," she replied, big gray eyes peering at him in a way that made him want to agree with anything she said. "But Rattlesnake is a small town. If the banks get wind that this isn't a real marriage, they may not think the collateral is real, either. I can't take a chance on losing that loan."

Too sleep deprived to argue further, he threw his hands up in surrender. "Okay. Okay. Have it your way. Plan a wedding in Westminster Cathedral for all I care."

What was he worrying about? Since this wedding of hers would never happen, let her plan anything her little heart desired. As long as she stuck around until Evan's mother was located, that was all he cared about. He had no intention of giving up his bachelor status.

Chapter Two

Kati moved in that afternoon.

"Is this all the stuff you got?" Cookie asked, peering into the trunk of her ancient green Toyota.

He'd come scuttling out the door the minute she'd arrived, offering his assistance. From all appearances, he was as relieved to have her here as Colt was.

Before the interview with Colt, when the old cook had first opened the door for her, Kati had been hard-pressed to hide her misgivings. She hadn't known whether to laugh or scream. Since her second arrival, the man had gone out of his way to be helpful, and she regretted judging him by his bizarre appearance.

"I travel light," Kati said in answer to his question about her lack of belongings.

In foster care there was never any time or place to collect "things." She'd learned at an early age not to cling to possessions, so traveling light came easy.

Cookie hoisted the two cardboard boxes while she

grabbed the battered plaid suitcase and several hangers of clothes. They carried everything inside in one trip.

Caesar, Kati's cat, insulted by the long car ride, twitched his long tail and marched into the house like royalty. Cookie shot him a questioning glance. "Boss know you got a cat?"

"Why? Is that a problem?" The sleek gray cat with aristocratic airs had been her companion for four years.

"Boss hates cats."

"Oh, dear." Biting her lip, she paused in the natural-stone entryway and frowned.

"Now, don't you worry none." A beefy hand patted awkwardly at her shoulder. "Just keep the critter out from underfoot and everything will be just fine. Colt's out of the house more than he's in, anyway."

"Okay," she murmured feebly, following Cookie and the insulted cat through a massive living room, then down a long hallway. She couldn't afford to make Colt angry, but Caesar was her family. She just hoped she could keep the independent animal out of the way.

"Boss figured as how you'd want to be close to the baby." Cookie stopped at the end of a long hallway dotted with bedrooms, lowered the boxes and pushed the golden-oak door inward.

Kati almost lost her breath as she entered a room beautifully decorated in restful greens. The furniture, the same golden oak she'd noticed throughout the ranch house, gleamed with a fresh shine, and a bouquet of spring flowers waited invitingly on the bedside table along with several magazines and a Bible. Staking his claim at once, Caesar leaped onto the thick sage comforter, circled twice and lay down, his yellow eyes daring anyone to protest.

"Why, Mr. Cookie, everything looks so lovely."

Dropping the bag, Kati went immediately to press her face into the fragrant pink flowers. "Did you pick these yourself?"

Dragging his gaze from the cat to Kati, the old man looked genuinely pleased at the compliment. "I told the boss you'd like them flowers. And I ain't Mr. Cookie. Everybody just calls me plain old Cookie."

At the mention of Colt, Kati's mouth went dry. He hadn't come out to greet her when she'd arrived, though that didn't come as any surprise. He had a ranch to run, and from the looks of things, he'd been too busy with Evan to get much work done. Still, she wondered what he must be thinking now that the enormity of their agreement had had time to sink in. She sucked in a deep breath.

"Where is 'the boss'?"

"Getting some shut-eye. Once you got the baby to sleeping good, that little critter ain't never woke up. Colt figured he could do with some catching up of his own."

"He did look tired."

"I've seen that boy stay up for days on end when he was rodeoing. Drive all day, rodeo all night." The old cook chuckled and rubbed his scruffy chin. "But that baby boy's done got him whupped."

Kati grinned at the thought of Colt letting anything get the best of him. To her, he was invincible. Taking in a homeless baby and agreeing to a marriage of convenience for that baby's sake only proved the point.

"Where is the baby's room?"

"Next one down." He gestured vaguely and started out the door. "You just go on and make yourself to home, Miss Kati. I got some pies in the oven." He disappeared around the corner only to reappear again immediately. "What's your favorite pie?"

"Apple."

"Hot dang! I knowed I liked you. Apple it is."

Kati smiled as the massive cook disappeared once more, thankful for a sensitive nose that had picked up the scent of apples and cinnamon as soon as she'd entered the back door.

Though anxious to put away her things and explore the sprawling ranch house, Kati's first thoughts were of Evan. When she'd left him several hours ago he'd been contentedly sleeping in Colt's arms. By now a hungry tummy should be waking him.

At the end of the hall she discovered two doors instead of the expected one. Unsure of which held the nursery she quietly pushed open the one on the right.

A king-size bed dominated a room decorated in turquoise and black and more of the golden-oak furniture. Sprawled across the thick black comforter was none other than the boss himself, Colt Garret. Kati's foolish heart gave a lurch as she stood glued to the spot, staring at him.

He was as magnificent in repose as he was awake. One long arm was flung upward mussing his dark hair. Lines of fatigue radiated around his eyes. His mouth hung open, the firm, sensuous lips relaxed and inviting. Kati couldn't take her eyes off those lips.

For long moments she gaped, willing herself to leave and not a bit surprised when she couldn't. He'd kissed her once a long time ago in high school, and though he clearly didn't remember, she'd never forgotten the warm, firm feel of that mouth. He'd come off the football field in exuberant victory, picked her up and twirled her around, then kissed her soundly before disappearing in a sea of shouting, screaming fans. He'd probably done that a thousand times to a thousand girls, but for Kati it was a defining moment in her life.

Over the years, fantasies of Colt had sustained her through a bleak parade of countless foster homes. With each new place, she'd curl up in some quiet spot and pretend Colt was coming to get her. At last she'd have someone to love her forever. That was the best thing about fantasies. In her constant moves, she had to leave people, places and things, but never Colt. He was permanently with her, if only in her heart. Even now, as a grown woman who knew better than to indulge in fantasies, the teenage memory came back warm and inviting.

She wanted to go to him, lie down on that bed beside him, press her lips to his and feel their magic once again. She might very well have done it, if young Mr. Evan Parker hadn't chosen that exact moment to awaken, his cry ripping the quiet with the force of a jackhammer.

Startled into action, Kati backed into the hall, but not before Colt also awakened. Sexy, sleepy brown eyes locked with hers seconds before she beat a hasty retreat toward the nursery.

Colt struggled upward from a heavy slumber. Somewhere a baby cried. The heavy weight of responsibility pressed in on him. A baby. The baby needed him. He had to get there. Through sheer force of will he yanked his protesting eyelids upward. A woman stood at the end of his bed.

Hell's bells, the whole world had gone berserk. Babies crying. Women skulking around.

Colt leaped off the bed only to stumble over his own

boots. With a vicious kick he sent them sailing across the room where they thudded against the pale green wall. The pain in his toe radiated to his brain, jolting him to wakefulness. Confusion cleared, and memory returned. Evan was calling him.

Heart still pounding, toe throbbing, he limped across the hall to the nursery. The door stood open, and the new nanny was bent over Evan's crib, talking softly as her hands busily changed his diaper. So that's who'd been in his room. He wondered why.

Colt stood outside the door and watched her, anxious that she do a good job. Evan was a sweet little critter who'd gotten under Colt's skin more than he wanted to admit. And if Miss Loony Toon didn't do right by the boy, she'd be out the door by sundown.

Once the baby was changed Kati disappeared into the bathroom, washed her hands and returned to scoop Evan into her arms. His crying became a high-pitched wail Colt recognized as hunger.

"Time for a bottle," he said, lounging against the door frame.

Kati jumped and spun around. Her face flushed bright red. "I...I...where are they?"

He hitched his chin in the direction of the hall. "Come on, I'll show you. Cookie has a supply already fixed."

He led the way into the kitchen, removed a bottle from the refrigerator and quickly warmed it in the microwave. Three weeks of child care had taught him more than he'd ever wanted to know about a baby's needs.

After shaking a bit of milk onto his wrist, he determined it safe and reached for Evan. "I'll feed him."

"I can do it." Grabbing the bottle, she turned abruptly and sailed out of the kitchen.

Colt frowned, watching the sway of her long, dark hair as she scuttled down the hall like a frightened kitten. What was that all about?

He followed her back to the nursery where she sat in the rocker holding Evan.

"What were you doing in my room?" he asked as abruptly as she'd left the kitchen.

She blushed deeply, and the color bathed her pale skin in a downright appealing pink.

"Well, I wasn't stealing the silver," she replied stiffly. "Having only just arrived, I was trying to locate the nursery."

Her rigid voice and stiff back said she was offended. He hadn't accused her of anything, but she seemed to think he had. Was that the problem? She thought he was checking up on her? Well, he was, wasn't he? For Evan's sake.

Face averted, she turned her attention to the baby. A long strand of chestnut-colored hair fell over her shoulder onto the baby. Holding Evan with one hand while balancing the bottle with her chin, Kati used the free hand to gather the smooth, dark tresses into a ponytail which she then drew over her opposite shoulder.

Colt followed the action, thinking what beautiful hair she had. This afternoon she'd been groomed like a businesswoman with one of those sleek up-dos. Somewhere since he'd seen her last, she'd changed into jeans and a T-shirt and let down her long, glorious hair.

She wasn't what he'd consider a particularly beautiful woman, but she exuded a kind of feminine grace he found uniquely alluring. She wore little makeup, but her skin was clear and soft looking, her lips full and gently curving. Thick black lashes framed a pair of large gray eyes and cast shadows against her cheeks.

But it was the long mane of hair that drew him most. If he took two steps he could touch it, feel the silky fullness on his skin. Maybe even press his nose into the clean fresh scent. One hand, as if acting on its own, started to reach out.

Hell's bells! He snapped the offending hand down to his side. What had gotten into him? This woman was a temporary nanny—with the emphasis on temporary. It was bad enough he'd let her trick him into signing that confounded paper. He could easily have loaned her the money or been her cosigner instead of promising to marry her, but fatigue had kept him from seeing through her ridiculous plan. She was either crazy, desperate or a gold digger, and he must be completely out of his mind to think about touching her.

But he was okay. He could deal with the entire mess. As long as she took good care of Evan, and let him go on with his life, he'd be happy. Signing that paper meant nothing. She'd be out of here long before a month was up.

He glanced back at the woman, expecting deceit to be written on her like a neon sign. No such luck. Totally attuned to the infant in her arms, she looked like the Madonna.

Colt jerked at the notion. There he went again. Annoyed and frustrated, he muttered gruffly, "I've got work to do. Supper's at six." Then he stomped out of the room.

Supper proved to be a sumptuous feast. Kati, tense as a fiddle string, sat across from Colt watching him shovel in enough chicken-fried steak, mashed potatoes and gravy to kill a horse, while Cookie shuffled about the kitchen, sweat glistening on his cornrowed brow.

Kati took a deep drink from a tall glass of iced tea, savoring the cool sweetness as she savored the image of her employer. Though he looked more rested now than he had earlier, and a sight more chipper, he was every bit as handsome and rugged. Her stomach did a double axle and a triple flip just looking at him. The attraction grew with every glance, an attraction she'd work hard to ignore given the circumstances. Men in general, especially hunks like Colt Garret, didn't find her the least bit attractive. And even if they did, she wasn't interested in any more temporary relationships in her life. Kati's Angels would be permanent, would give her roots and stability, the three things she'd always wanted. She wasn't about to stick her heart out on her sleeve for someone to rip to shreds. Still, looking at Colt wouldn't be a problem, and tonight she wanted to look her fill.

"You get settled in all right?" he asked congenially, aiming his rich-chocolate gaze in her direction.

"Fine, thank you." Her lips felt as stiff as new shoes. They'd gotten off to such a bad start that afternoon, she wasn't sure what to expect.

"Baby asleep?"

"Oh, yes," she answered around a bite of buttery mashed potatoes. In the past ten minutes, she'd stuffed herself like a Charles Dickens orphan. "A baby his age sleeps a lot."

"Not when I was taking care of him," Colt answered wryly.

His cute smile set off another chain of flips and somersaults that Kati battled by drowning them in cold tea. But his smile was a welcome change, considering what happened that afternoon in the nursery. Colt had clearly thought she was snooping. Well, she had been, hadn't she? But only by accident. As a teenager, she'd once been falsely accused of stealing from a foster family. Though she'd eventually been cleared, the cloud of suspicion had hovered and she'd never quite forgotten the bitter humiliation of such an accusation. Colt already thought she was a lunatic; she couldn't allow him to think she was a thief, as well.

Cookie appeared with a steaming apple pie and interrupted her anxious musings.

"Got some ice cream to go with this, too, Miss Kati." He slid the pan onto a trivet close to Kati's elbow, bringing the cinnamon scent right beneath her nose.

"Hey," Colt said, pretending hurt, "what about me? Don't I get some pie and ice cream?"

"Ladies first," Cookie insisted, sliding a saucer of pie in Kati's direction. "Ain't every day we have a guest as perty and nice as this one, and I want to make sure you and your cranky attitude don't run her off."

"Cranky? I'm not cranky." He turned to Kati, hands spread in teasing supplication. "Have I been cranky today?"

She laughed. "You? Never." But he *had* been cranky. Frantic, funny and so sexy she could melt like a chocolate bar on the dashboard.

Cookie's air-horn laugh blasted. "This one got your number in a hurry, boy. Better watch out."

Suddenly the rotund cook froze and cast a wary eye toward the doorway. "Uh-oh."

Following his gaze, Colt stiffened. Slowly he raised his fork and pointed. "What in blazes is that?"

Caesar, tail twitching, pranced regally into the dining room as if to say, "You started dinner without me?"

Kati grimaced. Great. Leave it to the recalcitrant cat to make a grand entrance the very first night. "Caesar. Come here, boy." Kati patted the side of her leg, hoping against hope that for once in his life, he'd obey.

The cat ignored her, making a beeline for Colt instead. "You didn't tell me you had a cat." He sounded as though she had leprosy instead of a pet.

"Sorry. I never thought…"

"I'm not exactly a cat hater," he said slowly. "But in my book cats were put on this earth for one purpose—alligator bait."

Kati didn't know if he was serious or kidding. "I'll keep him in my room," she said hurriedly. "He won't bother you."

Making a liar out of her, Caesar chose that moment to begin a slow, seductive weave through Colt's legs. The cowboy glared down at him. "Cats belong in the barn."

Caesar sat and raised a plaintive paw to Colt's knee. Suspiciously the cowboy drew back. "What's he doing?"

Why, oh, why had she spoiled her cat by feeding him from the table? Kati made a face and in a small voice said, "I think he wants a piece of your steak."

"My steak! Not a chance." After a second, more-insistent pat from Caesar's paw, Colt ripped off a bite of the meat and jabbed it in the general direction of the cat, muttering, "Anything to make him go away. Blasted feline."

As Cookie sounded his air-horn laugh once again, Caesar carefully, daintily took the offering between his teeth and retired to the corner to dine.

Between bites, Colt kept an anxious eye on the corner. Finally he frowned and said, ''I hope that's not a tomcat. They roam, you know, and caterwaul all hours of the night.''

''No, no. Don't worry. He's not a tomcat. Caesar's been neutered.''

Cookie stopped dead in his tracks, turned and gazed at the cat. Colt swallowed hard and did the same. Then the two men looked at each other in horror.

''Poor guy,'' Colt commiserated, casting a long sympathetic look toward the animal.

''Yeah,'' Cookie breathed, then rushed back into the kitchen as though the same fate awaited him if he stuck around any longer.

''Well,'' Colt twisted uncomfortably in his chair. ''Since the poor critter doesn't have much else to live for, I guess he can stay. But he's confined to your room. Understand? I can't abide a cat underfoot.''

''Absolutely. That's fine. No problem. Thank you so much,'' she gushed. Shut up, Kati. Stop gushing as though he's handed you the winning lottery ticket. But her relief was genuine. She couldn't let anything happen to good old Caesar. He was all the family she had.

In her rush of gratitude, Kati leaned forward and placed her hands on the tabletop. The fingertips of one hand made inadvertent contact with the hot pie plate.

''Oh!'' she cried out, yanking the burned hand to her chest.

Instantly, Colt was beside her. He pulled her fingers into his and pressed them against his lips for two quick kisses.

Shocked, Kati didn't know what to do, but her heart reacted violently. No one had ever kissed her fingers.

Certainly not a gorgeous man she barely knew who made her heart flutter by just being in the same room.

As soon as Colt realized what he'd done, he froze, blinked at her fingers in confusion, then plunked them into her tea glass. The icy plunge shocked her back to her senses.

"There. That should take the edge off." Releasing her as though he'd been the one burned, Colt backed around to his chair. After a moment's silence he cleared his throat. "If you get blisters, Cookie has some ointment that might help."

"I'm fine, really. More surprised than hurt." She was surprised all right but not by the hot plate. Kati withdrew her fingers from the glass and laid them in her lap, the gentle heat of Colt's mouth lingering much longer than the burn.

An uncomfortable silence hovered over the table until Colt ripped off a bite of hot buttered bun and leaned toward her. "Say, do you ride? I've got plenty of gentle horses if you're interested."

Clearly, Colt was eager to guide the conversation to safer ground.

"I love to ride," she admitted, struggling to concentrate on horses when all she could think of was Colt's mouth against her skin. "Though I'm not very good at it."

"Wes Patterson's wife, Becky, is an expert rider. She comes out twice a week to do my bookkeeping. I'll bet she wouldn't mind showing you around."

"What about them college gals, boss?" Cookie poked his head around the corner. "They'll be coming soon and Miss Kati could ride out with them. They ain't much use for nothing else."

"College students?" Kati's curiosity piqued.

Nodding, Colt jabbed a fork into his pie and held it aloft, letting ice cream drip onto the saucer as he spoke. "Every summer we take on a few agri-business interns from the university. We get some cheap help during a busy time and they gain a summer of living and working on a real ranch. Works out pretty well for all of us."

"Hmpf." Cookie whipped into the room to whisk the emptied dishes from the table. "Half-baked greenhorns is more of a nuisance than a help."

"Everybody has to start somewhere, Cookie."

Impressed and touched that Colt generously allowed greenhorns the opportunity for hands-on ranching experience, Katie couldn't help smiling when Cookie barked back as he retreated into the kitchen. "I never said they didn't. As long as they stay out of my kitchen, we do fine."

With a chuckle, Colt winked at Kati. "The students we get out here would rather muck out barns than cook a meal. I think his kitchen's safe. But the offer still stands. Anytime you want to take a horse out, just let me know. I'll arrange for someone to ride with you until you feel comfortable on your own."

Fingers tingling, insides warming with each kind word, Kati said, "As much as I'd like to, I doubt I'll have the opportunity. Evan will take up all my time."

Colt waved off the worry. "Ah, Cookie can watch him sometime when he's napping."

Once again Cookie appeared. "I ain't no baby-sitter. Don't know a thing about young'uns."

Carrying a cup of coffee, the rotund cook scraped back a chair and settled his bulk next to Kati.

"Don't let him fool you, Kati," Colt said with an

ornery grin. "I've caught him in the nursery a few times."

"Some dumb cowboy was off somewhere and the little critter was crying." With a huff of disapproval, Cookie folded his tree-trunk arms atop his generous belly. "I couldn't leave the boy like that."

"Feeds him mashed potatoes, too," Colt whispered conspiratorially. "If we leave Evan with him too much, they'll be sporting matching bellies."

Enjoying the joke, Kati eyed the cook's sailing battleship with a grin. "Just as long as he doesn't get the tattoo to go with it."

As soon as the teasing words popped out, Kati covered her lips with her fingers, aghast. Had she offended the kindhearted old cook?

For two eternal heartbeats both men stared at her, surprised. Then they looked at each other and nearly fell out of their chairs laughing.

The tight muscles in Kati's neck eased as she joined them.

"I told you she's a good one," Cookie said.

Eyes dancing with laughter, Colt sat back in his chair and smiled at her.

Her accursed heart began another, most unwelcome, round of gymnastics. In the interest of self-preservation, experience had taught her to keep emotions firmly in check. But this time her heart paid no attention at all.

Over the years she'd been in enough new places to know how to make herself at home, but Colt Garret, with his innate kindness and warm humor, made her feel welcome. And it was the scariest feeling she'd ever experienced.

Chapter Three

Evan's screams jolted Kati upright in bed, sending a disgruntled Caesar flying. Scurrying into her robe, she glanced at the clock and rushed across the hall to the nursery. Two hours of sleep again tonight. Little surprise that her head ached and her legs moved like blocks of concrete. Since her arrival Evan had kept her awake most of every night suffering bouts of colic.

No wonder Colt had been so exhausted he'd agreed to marry her.

Anxious not to awaken the entire household, Kati scooped the stiff, squalling child into her arms, rushed to the kitchen for a bottle—which the baby refused to take—and slipped out the back door as quietly as possible.

The rich butter of summer moonlight lit the grassy backyard, and the stars were so bright and near she could see plainly. She paced the yard, jouncing and bouncing, singing and patting, while Evan suffered the misery of colic. Each time she thought he was settling, and started toward the house and precious sleep, the crying began again. Having no other way to ease him broke her heart.

"Poor little man," she crooned to Evan's contorted face. "You must hurt so bad."

The cool summer grass was damp with dew, so Kati took an old blanket from the patio, spread it on the ground and lowered her exhausted body. In the warm night air, frogs trilled and the scent of honeysuckle wafted in gentle waves.

The back door opened and she turned to see Colt silhouetted in the doorway. Quietly easing the door shut behind him, he came across the patio toward Kati and Evan. Kati's heart lurched. Bare-chested and bare-footed, he'd pulled on a pair of jeans without bothering with the top snap. His hair was disheveled and a five o'clock shadow had deepened the color of his cheeks so that he looked dark and dangerous and incredibly sexy.

"Boy sick again?" His quiet baritone carried on the still night air.

She nodded. To prove the point, Evan's voltage went from whimper to wail.

"He's miserable." Kati laid him on his back and tenderly stroked the rigid tummy. The baby's legs thrashed, but the wail eased to a fussy whimper. He gnawed repeatedly on his fist.

Colt hunkered down beside them. "Can't the doctor give him anything for this?"

"I don't know." Kati's braid fell forward and she tossed it back, suddenly self-conscious to have the half-dressed Colt so near. "Have you taken him for a checkup?"

Colt blinked at her, bewildered. "Hadn't even thought of it."

"We need to do that soon. He probably should start his immunizations."

"Yeah." He eased onto the blanket beside her. "Why don't you give Doc Armstrong a call tomorrow and set up an appointment?"

"Okay." With all her might, Kati concentrated on Evan. Not that it worked with Colt's living, breathing body only inches away. Fortunately, he was watching her hands massage and soothe the fussy baby, but when he tilted his head, turning his full attention to Kati, her breath jammed in her throat. "You been coming out here every night?"

"I didn't want to disturb anyone." She fidgeted with Evan's pajamas with one hand while the other patted and soothed. "Sorry if I woke you."

"Not your fault. And Evan sure can't help it." His gorgeous lips tilted in a smile. "Good thing the mosquitoes aren't out yet. They'd eat you alive."

Kati replied with a tremulous smile. "If coming out here helps Evan and lets you sleep, I'd still do it. You need your rest to run a ranch this large."

"Yeah. Well." He stretched his shoulders upward and rolled his head from side to side. "You're doing a good job with Evan. I just want you to know I've noticed, and I appreciate it."

A purl of pleasure lifted some of Kati's exhaustion. "He's a wonderful baby most of the time."

"Don't go getting attached." He said the words lightly, casually as if he meant them for himself as well as for her, but Kati needed the reminder. Evan was fast winning her heart.

"Don't worry. I know better than that." Relation-

ships were unfailingly temporary, as every foster kid
learned early on. That's why Kati's Angels was so important. The wonderful place filled with children who
needed her would be permanent in a way nothing else
ever had been. She was sorry Colt felt trapped by their
marriage contract, but someday he'd understand all the
good that would come of it.

Long legs stretched out on the small quilt, Colt
propped himself up on one elbow and curled in toward
the baby. "My attorney should find Evan's mother any-
day now, and he'll be going home where he belongs."

"You really think so?"

He looked up at her. "Sure."

Kati's heart sank like a battleship. As much as she
wanted a real home and family for Evan, if the mother
showed up before the month was out, Kati would lose
her dream, her chance for one permanent thing in her
life.

Colt shifted, bringing his warm, partially clad body
closer to Kati. The scent of clean sheets and lime soap
came with him. "You have to be tired of doing that,"
he murmured, motioning to her ever-massaging hands.

"It seems to help. See how he's beginning to relax?"

"Let me." He lifted her hand, replacing it with his
own. A delicious fluttering began in Kati's stomach at
the sight of Colt's cowboy-strong hands, large and dark
against the small baby's blue-fleece bunny pajamas. The
picture was beautiful, moving. She couldn't look away.

The baby sighed deeply, his little arms and legs going
limp, and Kati couldn't help thinking, Lucky baby, as
Colt's hands worked a magic rhythm.

"I think you've got the touch," she said.

"Yeah?" Colt looked pleased. "I never thought he
liked me."

Kati grinned at the admission. Who wouldn't like Colt Garret? "I think he's finally comfortable enough to sleep."

Colt withdrew his hand and sat up, resting on his heels.

"It's late. Maybe we can all get a little shut-eye before the sun comes up." Very gently he lifted the baby and stood, cradling the child in one arm while he extended the other to Kati. She knew touching him was a mistake, but she just couldn't help herself. Taking his hand, she let him pull her up until she was no more than a breath away from his naked chest. Moonlight gilded them, the cowboy, the sleeping baby and the nanny. The nanny, she had to remind herself. She was only and forever the nanny.

Colt rinsed the day's grime from his body and stepped out of the shower, eager to collapse in his big leather recliner and catch the farm market news and tomorrow's weather report. If rain didn't come soon, the wheat wouldn't grow, livestock prices would fall and his profits would decline for the second year in a row. Not that a bad year would break him, but he was in this thing for money, not love.

At the thought of love, he came up short, whisked the oversize white towel across his body, leaving his skin damp and drippy, and stepped into clean jeans and T-shirt. Love was not an emotion that impressed him much. Hadn't his sister been "in love" at least a dozen times now with a string of ex-loves so long he'd stopped keeping track of her latest husband? And he didn't even remember when his parents had been married to each other. Nor his grandparents. The Garret family's notion of love and marriage consisted of two months of bliss followed by two years of fighting and divorce courts. Not his idea of a good time. He shuddered and headed for the living room.

A game show flickered across his big-screen TV. Legs curled beneath her, the nanny, wearing shorts and a tank top the color of a sunset, sat in his recliner. Evan lay on a blanket on the floor babbling to his feet, and that blasted cat snoozed next to the baby. As soon as Colt entered the room, Kati popped up, looking at him with her huge gray eyes. What was she doing in here? In his chair?

''I hope you don't mind...'' She indicated the TV as she vacated his chair and moved to the couch, folding her legs under her again. Dark circles rimmed her eyes.

Mind? He hated it. Having a woman and baby under his roof, in his care, made him uncomfortable in his own house. Especially her, with that crazy paper she'd gotten him to sign and those big eyes of hers and that amazing mane of hair.

To avoid the woman he went to the baby and hunkered down on the carpet. Evan abandoned his foot fetish and turned a thousand-watt smile, albeit toothless, upon Colt. ''The boy here still keeping you up all night?''

He let the baby take his finger and gnaw on it while the cat wound around his boots.

''Yes. But it's okay,'' she said quickly. ''He's a charmer when he's feeling good.''

Colt rattled a blue horse for Evan, then caught himself. What the heck was he doing? He slammed a hand through his damp hair and rose. ''You want a television for your room?''

Kati looked surprised. ''No, of course not. This is fine.''

Great. So now he had to sit here in the living room with her every night. Just great. "Oh, well, I just…you want some popcorn?" He didn't know where that came from.

After a moment's hesitation, during which she studied him quizzically, she replied, "Popcorn sounds good, actually, but I'll get it. You have to be tired after working all day in this heat."

"Are you saying Evan's not work?" He smiled ruefully. "He sure was to me."

Already moving toward the kitchen, Kati laughed, a sweet feminine sound as refreshing as summer rain. Her hair hung loose and damp as though she'd just washed it, and when she passed by, he caught the subtle hint of some flowery soap. The notion of Kati in the shower flickered through his head. He slammed the door on that thought so fast he got a headache.

By the time she returned, he'd settled into his chair and flipped the channels, an action that made him feel in control again. The muscles in the back of his neck were even starting to relax.

"I brought some iced tea, too." Somehow she balanced a bowl of savory-smelling popcorn between her side and bent elbow while carrying two glasses of tea. "There's some leftover cheesecake if you want it."

No, he didn't want it. He wanted her to go away and stop making him feel so domestic. Colt popped the recliner upright and took a glass. "Cookie doesn't object to you messing around in his kitchen?"

"Of course not. He's so sweet."

"Sweet? Are we talking about the same guy? The one who's tossed me out of my own house a half-dozen times for tracking in mud?"

"I clean up my mess."

He shot her a mock scowl. "Are you calling me a slob?"

Her eyes grew round and worried as though she'd insulted him. To show her he was joking and to wipe that look off her face, he tossed a piece of popcorn at her. "See, I'm not a slob."

As the popcorn hit the couch and bounced onto the floor Kati smiled. Relief shifted through him. He may not want her here but he sure didn't want her cowering like a kicked pup. "You like to play games?"

Dang! What he'd say that for? Kati's worried look returned. "Checkers, I mean."

"Oh, sure."

She looked baffled, and he felt stupid. Dang this situation. He'd talked coherently to a thousand women, bedded more than his share, and yet, the hired help had him tongue-tied like a schoolboy. If only he hadn't signed that paper. The notion of getting married had him all out of whack.

He stomped out of the room and returned with the checkerboard. Kati was bent over Evan, changing his diaper. Setting the checkers on the coffee table, Colt moved to her side and watched. "You make that look easy."

She smiled up at him and his stomach turned over. Must be that extra helping of enchilada he had at supper.

"Even the plastic ones take time to master."

"Tell me about it. I can't count the times those little tabs stuck to his skin instead of each other. And we won't even discuss what happens if you don't get the legs tight enough."

She grinned at him again and he grinned back, enjoying the moment in spite of himself. When she'd set-

tled the baby they moved to the couch, as if by prear-
rangement, to play checkers. Ten minutes into the game,
Colt knew he'd met his match.

Kati played with intensity, studying the board between each move for such a long time that Colt couldn't
resist teasing her.

"Are you plotting strategy or trying to move the
checkers by telekinesis?"

"Shh. I think I have it."

"I hope so. All this concentration's making me
thirsty. I need more tea."

Her head popped up. "I'll get it for you."

He forestalled her with an upraised palm. "No. You
decide your next move. I'll get my own tea. I'll even
bring you another glass if you'll just move."

He got up to get the drinks and when he returned she
was about to jump one of his kings. "Did you cheat
while I was gone?" he asked in stunned disbelief.

"I do not cheat," she answered indignantly.

"You do, too. When I left this room this king was
here—" he realigned the checkers, purposely taking the
advantage "—and yours was here."

"They were not." She switched them back.

"Were, too. Weren't they, Evan?" He looked toward
the infant who gooed a reply.

"See?" he told her.

"Shame on you, Colt Garret, forcing an innocent
child to lie for you."

Colt laughed out loud at that one, then scattered the
checkers helter-skelter, totally destroying the game. Kati
laughed, too, and slapped his hands. For one long moment they sat smiling into each other's eyes. With a
start, Colt realized he liked Kati Winslow. He really
liked her. And that would never do.

"Well," he said as he stood uncomfortably and rubbed both hands down the thighs of his jeans. "Guess I'll call it a night."

"Me, too. Evan still needs a bath before his last bottle. Thanks for the checker game." Hair swinging around her, she gathered the baby in her arms and arched a teasing eyebrow. "Even if you do cheat."

Once she disappeared around the corner, murmuring sweet nonsense to Evan, Colt sighed and flopped into the recliner, burying his face in his hands.

Where, oh, where, was Natosha Parker?

Kati leaned over the infant tub, gently washing Evan's hair, her mind swirling from the strange evening with her employer. For those few minutes over the checkerboard, they'd laughed and had fun as if they'd been friends for a long time, though her heart had pounded at her rib cage like a battering ram every time he brushed against her or shot that incredible grin in her direction.

"He's a nice man, Evan, though he probably doesn't want us to think that." Any more than she wanted to think it. Keeping a distance emotionally from the appealing Mr. Garret was very important. Living under the same roof, eating at the same table, bumping each other in the hallways was bad enough. If she let her lonely heart join forces with her runaway imagination she'd end up crazy about a man who only wanted her gone. And she'd learned a long time ago to guard her heart against emotional attachments. If she didn't care too much, the inevitable parting didn't hurt so badly.

The baby gooed, splashing her, a reminder of another fast-developing emotional bond. Regardless of Colt's warning that she not get attached, Kati struggled constantly against the tide of feeling Evan evoked. She could love him, all right, as long as she remembered that he was only passing through her life. Just like Colt.

As she dried and dressed the infant, Kati kissed his tiny fingers and toes, the rush of maternal love too strong to ignore. How could any mother have abandoned a child so precious?

"If you were mine, no power on earth could keep us apart."

But he wasn't hers and thinking such a thing frightened her. What would she do when the time came to give him up?

Hugging her temporary baby close, she settled into the rocker and fed him, watching as his lids grew heavy and sleep overwhelmed him. With a kiss, she placed him in his crib, covering him with a petal-soft blanket.

Tiptoeing to her room, she undressed and tumbled into bed hoping for a few hours' rest before the nightly ritual of walking in the moonlight began. She'd been foolish to spend so much time playing checkers with Colt, but she couldn't have slept, anyway, until Evan did.

With a weary sigh she closed her eyes. A movie of Colt cheating at checkers, grinning his ornery grin, played behind them. She wanted the vision to go on forever.

Caesar circled around her feet several times, looking for just the right spot. Long before he settled, Kati was fast asleep.

Sometime later she stretched awake in the still-darkened room, smiling at some lovely dream. Only the hum of central air broke the quiet. Unsure what had awakened her, she rolled toward the bedside digital. A large red *4:00* stared back.

Evan! She jerked upright, adrenaline bursting through every cell. Why hadn't he awakened? Was he all right? Or was he awake, screaming in pain, and she'd been too tired and distracted by dreams of Colt to hear him?

Throwing the sheet aside, she bolted from the bed, dislodging the cat. On bare feet she flew down the hall and into the nursery, pulling up short at the sight before her.

Dimly lit by a blue horseshoe night-light, Colt sat in the rocker holding Evan. One long, bare foot tapped the floor to keep the chair moving.

"Is he all right? Has he been crying?" Even to her own ears she sounded panicky.

Colt glanced up and lifted a finger to his lips. "He's settling down nicely," he whispered.

"I didn't even hear him."

"Guess that checker game was too much for you."

Kati's anxiety shot up a notch. Was that condemnation in his tone? "I'm terribly sorry. Let me take him so you can go back to bed."

"He's out now. I'll put him down." The rocker slowed, and Colt eased upward. "Looks like he's finally beaten this colic thing. All I did was give him the bottle and he went right back to sleep."

Colt's tall, lean frame filled the room. He looked as out of place among the baby furniture as a stallion at high tea. When he placed the sleeping child in the crib, Kati saw that he'd come to the nursery in a hurry just as she had.

His hair was mussed, as she knew hers must be, and he was shirtless. The naked muscles of his back and arms flexed as he covered the baby and straightened.

Mouth dry, Kati tried not to stare at the beautiful man standing so near. She stepped to the crib and looked down at the baby. Given the dream she'd just had, look-ing at Colt was deadly.

"I really am sorry he woke you," she tried again.

He glanced her way. In the soft light she caught the hint of a smile. "It's okay. This once."

She supposed that was his way of letting her know that Evan was her job.

Evan stirred. Both adults fell silent as they gazed down. The baby pulled his knees beneath him and shoved his bottom in the air. His lips made sucking motions. Briefly he squirmed, searching until his curled fist found his mouth. The soft fragrance of baby lotion emanated from his warm body.

Something about the innocent child and the dark room created an air of intimacy. Kati could almost be-lieve that Evan belonged to her and the man standing in his bare feet next to her. Considering the deal they'd made, hers was a dangerous fantasy. If she had any sense at all, she'd go back to bed right now.

Pivoting to leave, her foot caught his much larger one, and she stumbled. A strong hand shot out to steady her. They were an eyelash apart, so close in fact that Kati saw the rise and fall of Colt's wide, tanned chest.

"Kati," he whispered. He, too, must have felt the tenderness in the air, for he pulled her close. The heady scent of man and shower soap assaulted her senses.

His rough cowboy hands slid up her arms. Goose bumps prickled her skin. He noticed and smoothed his palms up and down over the flesh.

Kati moistened her lips and swallowed hard, sud-denly aware of her scantily clad body. Her heart banged wildly. "We'd better get some sleep."

"Yeah."

But neither moved.

In the shadowed room, Colt's brown eyes questioned hers.

"Kati," he whispered again.

The sound of her name on his lips sent shivers through her. The gooseflesh returned and brought their friends.

"Cold?" he asked.

"No." She hardly recognized the shaky voice that was her own.

"Ah."

With that tiny sound he acknowledged the real reason for her shivering. Slowly, slowly, giving her the option of escape, he pulled her toward him. His gaze locked on hers. A muscle twitched below his eye.

Like the proverbial moth to a flame, Kati went. Though her mind screamed against it, her heart couldn't resist. Hadn't she wondered what it would be like in Colt Garret's arms?

As she moved the last inch to press into his naked chest, the heat of his body welcomed her. She sighed and leaned into him, hating herself for being so weak. Getting this involved with Colt Garret could only bring disaster.

One strong arm wrapped around her waist, pulling her flush against his hardness. The other came up to stroke her hair, smoothing it over her shoulder.

"You have beautiful hair," he murmured.

She had no answer, no glib reply to break the magic spell that was Colt. His nearness was an intoxicant. A rush of longing sent her heart into arrhythmia. Her skin tingled deliciously with tiny pulses of electricity until every nerve ending seemed to scream Colt's name. She could scarcely breath.

"Colt, I—"

He laid a finger across her lips. Little by little, he lowered his head, still watching her, gauging her for— she didn't know what. Like a stunned doe, she watched him in return, fascinated by the shadows playing along the handsome planes and angles of his face. In the next moment he replaced the finger with his lips—a mere whisper of a kiss that left her straining for more.

He groaned softly and drew back, though his arms still held her.

It was a good thing, too, because Kati was sure if he released her, she'd crumble to the floor and melt into the carpet like ice cream in the Texas sun. Though her annoying conscience kept saying she was crazy to put herself in this situation, the rest of her was awash in such incredible sensations that she could have stood there all night staring into Colt's whisker-stubbled face. So what if she had vowed never again to give anyone a chance to reject her. So what if she only came here to secure her future. So what if the marriage they planned was only temporary. To Kati none of those things registered.

Fortunately, Colt had better sense. He released her reluctantly, holding her only with his intense brown gaze. Several heartbeats passed, pulsing in the sweet electricity of the room before Colt sighed heavily, pulled a hand down his face and backed slowly out of the room.

Chapter Four

"Come on, Jace," Colt shouted into the telephone. "This is getting real serious. Surely you've found some trace of this Natosha Parker person."

"Sorry, Colt, I wish I could give you better news. The paper trail stops with the attorney who prepared the custody forms. He claims he'd never seen her before or since, and I have no reason to distrust that."

Colt throttled the phone. This thing was getting out of hand, and as much as he hated to admit it, he was getting scared. He couldn't be a daddy, and he sure as heck couldn't be a husband. If last night's fiasco was anything, it was a warning. This had to end—and end soon.

He stalked to the wide bay window in his office and opened the blind, looking out at his back lawn. At the sight before him, he started to sweat.

Kati sat on the patio swing with Evan in her arms. Her lips moved, smiling at the boy as she raised him high above her and wiggled his body in the air. He must have laughed because her expression changed to that of wonder. She lowered him to her shoulder and hugged him tightly, the smile on her lips as gentle as snowfall. Evan's little fist latched on to a lock of her stunning hair. Katie reached up and carefully untwined the chubby, grasping fingers.

The May sun, not yet unmerciful, cast red highlights into that captivating mane of dark hair. She'd pulled it up on the sides, out of the baby's reach, but with her every movement, the long locks swept forward.

Colt remembered the way her hair felt in his hands— heck, he remembered the way *she* felt in his hands. Soft and trembling so that he'd nearly lost what was left of his mind.

Did women really tremble like that?

He'd replayed that scene a dozen times since last night, and it still didn't make sense. Had he started it? Had she? The whole episode put him into a state of panic, elevated by the fact that Evan's mother was no-where to be found.

As much as he'd enjoyed that kiss with Miss Kati Winslow, the fact remained she wanted something he couldn't give. In only a matter of time now she'd hit him with that stupid paper he'd signed. Maybe she'd been working up to that very thing last night. If he and Jace didn't find Evan's mother very soon—well, the result was just too awful to think about. Every Garret that had ever lived hurt himself and everyone around when he got married. He couldn't, wouldn't, do that to a nice girl like Kati.

Kati chose that moment to stand. Evan on one hip, she reached around to straighten the leg of her shorts. Colt's belly tightened as he followed the action, staring out the window like a voyeur at the nanny's round bottom and smooth slender legs. Long legs. Legs he'd noticed last night when she'd stumbled into the nursery wearing only a T-shirt and panties. The burning in his gut moved lower. Hell's bells, he hoped she'd been wearing panties.

He spun away from the glass and barked into the receiver, "What about a private investigator?"

Thirty minutes later as he labored over the ranch's financial records, wishing he'd had sense enough to let his bookkeeper Becky teach him how to use his own computer, someone knocked at the door. Knowing his caller had to be Kati—Cookie never knocked anywhere except at "Miss Kati's door"—he braced himself.

"Come in."

The door opened and Kati entered. Her eyes flickered to his face, then down to the baby in her arms. After last night she must be dreading this moment as much as he was.

She licked her lips. Just a quick flash of pink tongue that left her mouth moist and shining. He had a flashback of her doing the same thing last night. The action was unsettling, and he wished to Pete she'd stop it. His gut clenched and his palms grew moist.

"What do you want?" He hadn't intended to be so abrupt, but the question stood. What did she want with him, anyway?

"Did you forget about Evan's appointment?"

Oh, great. He smacked the ink pen down with enough force to make the baby jump. Today was Evan's doctor's appointment.

"Can't you take him?"

"Not this time. You'll have to sign papers giving permission for medical treatment. After that, they'll probably let me bring him in."

"Terrific." He slammed the ledger closed and stood, none too pleased. Spending time with Kati and Evan was not a good thing. "I have enough work here to kill a horse, but I have to do your job, too."

The accusation was unfair, as he well knew, but life was not going his way lately, and he resented the fool out of it. And if Kati looked at him again with those sad kitten eyes or licked her lips, he was going to lose his mind. He shoved a hand through his hair in exasperation.

"I'm sorry to bother you." Kati drew up to her full height, which wasn't too impressive, considering he still had eight inches on her. Indignation quivered around her like an aura. "But this little boy is going to get the best care I can give him. It isn't his fault he's been dumped here like a stray pup. And it wasn't my fault that you kissed me last night, if that's what's making you so cranky."

One thing about the nanny, she wasn't afraid to grab the bull by the horns. All the irritation seeped out of Colt as he studied her stiff posture. This little gray-eyed kitten could get riled up like a wildcat over Evan.

Protective. That's what she was. As protective as a real mother. She hovered over the child, taking notes every time he smiled or turned over in the crib. She played with him, talked to him and proudly reported each developmental milestone. The next thought hit him with the force of a Brahma bull.

"Are you Evan's real mother?"

Kati blinked at him for a second before laughing. "No, I'm not Evan's mother, but I do understand his situation better than most people ever could."

"How so?"

"Can I explain on the way?"

Colt gave a grudging smile. "See, you're a bulldog about that boy. You'll have him spoiled rotten."

But Colt followed her out to the truck just the same.

Once the baby was strapped into his car seat and they'd started down the long, straight driveway, Colt, curious now, said, "Tell me what you meant about understanding Evan's situation better than most."

"I grew up in foster care. I never knew what happened to my parents. Never knew why they didn't want me." She glanced up at him, then let her gaze fall to the child. "But I do know what it's like to be thrust on people you don't even know."

So that accounted for the lost look in her eyes.

"Must have been tough growing up that way."

"Yeah. So you can understand why I want to make sure Evan never feels unwanted. And I hope—" she swallowed hard and stared out the side window "—I hope he knows someone loves him for no other reason than because he exists. Every child deserves that."

Colt's gut wrenched. He looked from the road to the woman and back again. Her face in profile, Kati stared out at the miles and miles of pastureland, probably not seeing any of the cowboys and farmers who touched their hats in greeting as the truck sped by them. There was no self-pity in her, but Colt wondered if she spoke of her own painful childhood as well as Evan's situation.

Against his better judgment, he reached across the seat and squeezed her hand.

"Evan's going to be okay," he assured her. "Everything possible is being done to find his mother."

"What if she doesn't want him?" She pivoted from the window, her expression worried. "Have you considered that?"

Sure he had. For the entire ten minutes he'd taken to convince himself that if Natosha Parker could be found, she'd welcome her baby with open arms.

Kati trailed a finger down Evan's arm. The baby responded with a happy kick. "There *could* be a good explanation for her leaving him, but I can't think of one. Can you?"

"Well, yeah. I thought maybe she'd gotten into trouble and had this baby without anyone to help her. Then maybe she needed time to get back on her feet financially. Once that was accomplished, she'd come for him."

"Is that really what you thought?"

"Sure it is." Wasn't it? Or had he created the pleasant little scenario to reassure himself that he was only a temporary daddy? Anxiety threatened to choke him. He didn't want to think about what would happen if Natosha Parker never returned.

By then they'd reached the low brick building with the sign out front reading Clinic. Colt wheeled the truck into a parking space and killed the motor.

"Here we are, kid," he said, turning in his seat. The baby reacted with a delighted gurgle and flung his arms toward Colt. With a shake of his head, Colt closed his eyes and sighed. Who could resist something so sweet? Lifting the baby from his carrier, he grinned and said, "What are you laughing at, boy? This is the doctor's office. You're gonna hate us for this."

Kati laughed, and Colt enjoyed the sound. But he didn't want to think about that, either.

He swung Evan into his arms and waited for Kati to get the diaper bag. She came around the truck, long hair swinging in that fetching way, and reached for the boy.

"I've got him." Colt grabbed his hat from the dash,

jabbed it onto his head and followed the swinging hair into the clinic. He'd never felt so domesticated in his life.

Kati roamed her pristine bedroom, straightening pictures that didn't need straightening and rearranging books on the bookshelf. Finally she collapsed into the stuffed chair beside her bed, procrastinating the inevitable confrontation. Caesar, stretched out in the sunshine beside her, cast her a curious glance and dozed off.

Now that Evan had adjusted to a normal schedule and slept all night, Kati knew she should get things organized for her building project. There was that plot of land to purchase, contractors to schedule, permits to apply for, but none of that could happen until she'd secured a loan. And that meant confronting Colt with his promise.

But since the day they'd taken Evan to the doctor, a friendly camaraderie had sprung up between them that she was reluctant to destroy. Relieved to find the child healthy and thriving, she and Colt had celebrated with an ice-cream sundae. Over mounds of hot fudge and whipped cream, she'd come to know Colt Garret in a way that made him much more real than her one girlhood memory. He'd told her with pride of how he'd built the ranch from a one-man operation out of a camper trailer to a spread that commanded respect all over Texas. He also told her of Jett, his partner-brother who rode the rodeo circuits and didn't come around for months on end. And he'd worried out loud about the wheat prices and the lack of rain, taking her into his confidence in a way that made her feel important.

In return, she'd told him a little about her childhood

and of watching him quarterback the Rattlesnake High School RidgeRattlers all those years ago.

"No," he'd said in disbelief, dangling a spoonful of vanilla ice cream in front of his sexy open mouth.

"Yes." A smile lifted the corners of her lips. "You were a senior. I, a lowly freshman."

"I thought your name sort of sounded familiar. We actually attended the same high school?"

"Only for that one year. Certainly not long enough for us to get acquainted. I attended five different high schools all over this part of Texas before finally graduating."

"I musta been cute for you to remember me," he said with a twinkle in his eye.

"Why, you conceited thing." She tapped his hand with the back of her spoon. "You were cute, and you knew it, too."

She didn't bother to say that he was much cuter now.

He chuckled softly. "I had the world by the tail back then."

"Every girl in school had a crush on you."

"Including you?"

Oops. She scooped in a bite of sweet cold chocolate to cool the heat rushing over her cheekbones.

"I was a foster kid, remember? I was never anywhere long enough to develop crushes."

It was almost the truth.

"Liar."

Kati looked up to see Colt grinning at her with sheer male conceit. "You had a crush on me."

"I did not."

"Not even a teeny-tiny one?" He pointed a spoon at her, daring her to lie.

"Well…"

"I knew it!" He grinned at Evan, holding out his ice-cream spoon for the baby to lick. "She had a killer crush on me, kid."

Kati watched the way Colt related to Evan and wondered if he realized how he'd automatically drawn the gurgling baby into their conversation. Or if he had any idea how much ice cream he'd slid into the baby's mouth from his own spoon.

"Even if I did have a very small crush on you, I was dreadfully shy and a mere freshman. You, on the other hand, were always surrounded by your harem."

"A harem? Now what would you know about me and the ladies?"

"You were a legend."

He liked that. His face lit up and his eyes danced. "Was I?"

"Yes, I'm surprised one of those pretty cheerleader types didn't lasso you with your own rope."

As soon as the words left her mouth, she wanted them back. From the way Colt's face closed up, she knew she'd reminded him of their agreement.

"I never wanted to be lassoed." He jabbed the spoon deep into the ice cream.

That one remark was the only damper on their outing. Now she'd let an entire month pass without so much as mentioning his agreement to marry her if Evan's mother had not returned.

She'd waited too long already, and as much as she wanted Evan to have his mother back, she needed to get started on Kati's Angels. Marrying Colt was her only chance to make that dream come true.

"Caesar, my friend." She curled her toes around the animal's tail. "It's time to get this show on the road."

Digging in her wallet, she extracted the agreement

Colt had signed. Carefully smoothing out the paper, she studied the words. He'd promised, in writing, to marry her—if she had the nerve to call him on it.

"Cookie," she called, heading for the kitchen to fill time while working up the courage to confront Colt.

She discovered the old cook standing in his usual spot at the center island, busily churning flour into the humid air, his ever-present apron generously dusted. He turned to greet her with a wave of a wooden spatula.

"Need something?"

"Just came to visit," she answered slowly, surveying the amazing number of filled pots, pans and bowls spread around the kitchen. "Though you look like you could use some help in here. What can I do?"

He bristled. The blackjack sprouts on his head fairly quivered with indignation. "Is there something wrong with the food?"

Kati blinked in surprise. Had she insulted him?

He shuffled over to stir some concoction boiling on the stove. "I can make enough chow for a hundred hands any day. Never needed any help before. 'Course, if you got complaints."

In the time she'd been here, Cookie had been a friend. She hadn't meant to insult his wonderful cooking, which, if anything, had actually improved with the influx of summer help and college students. Wanting to make amends, she followed him from the industrial-size stove to the walk-in refrigerator.

"Was there any of that chocolate cake left from supper last night? I've never tasted one so moist."

He jabbed a finger toward the counter. "Right over there. Help yourself."

She tried another tack. "Did you know Colt is afraid someone else will lure you away from here one day?"

"I ain't going nowhere," he said stiffly. "He knows that."

Well, so much for subtlety. "Cookie, I'm sorry if I hurt your feelings. You're the best cook in the world. I thought maybe you would teach me a few things."

The wild flurry of flour ceased. "You cain't cook?"

"Just frozen stuff and quick things. Not real cooking."

"Well, why didn't you say so?" He peered at her from beneath shaggy brows. "How come your ma never taught you to cook?"

So Colt hadn't told him.

"I grew up in lots of different foster homes." The admission sounded pathetic, embarrassing her, so she added, "I never was interested before."

Cookie considered her over the giant mound of bread dough. "I ain't much of a mama, but I can sure enough teach you to cook." He nudged his chin toward a long row of cabinets. "Aprons is over in that second drawer."

As she tied the apron around her waist, a strange lump rose in Kati's throat. She had the ridiculous notion that she might cry over something as mundane as peeling potatoes for her temporary family. Every day she spent on the Garret Ranch brought new emotions, but this feeling of family, of belonging, stirred a yearning inside that had to stop soon or she'd die when her time here was over for good. She simply could not allow herself to be hurt that way again.

By the time Evan awoke from his nap, Kati was bent over the oven removing a giant pan of scalloped potatoes. Sweat beaded her brow. Even with the central air-conditioning the kitchen was hot work, shooting her respect for Cookie up another notch. Somehow, with only the help of a weekly maid, the old guy managed to keep the entire ranch spotlessly clean and still find time to cook for the twenty-some cowboys and cowgirls working for Colt.

"I'll finish that up, Miss Kati," he said with a grin when Evan's cries rose to a shriek. "Sounds like your boy is calling you."

Kati nodded and removed her apron, folded it neatly and placed it on the counter. *Your boy.* Cookie had called Evan her boy. It was only an expression. She knew that. But the words did have a lovely sound.

Over the years she'd learned to hold back her heart, to avoid hurt. If she stuck around the Garret Ranch too long she could be in for the biggest heartbreak of all. She simply had to discuss the marriage agreement tonight. The sooner she and Colt were married and Kati's Angels was built, the sooner she could escape these frightening emotions.

"I don't want to get married." Colt paced the carpet of his study like a bull in a pen, snorting and pawing the ground. He felt trapped—smothered.

"Natosha Parker has not been found, and a month is long passed."

Kati's tone was reasonable, but to Colt she sounded like a crazy woman. How had he let her trick him into this? He shoved a hand through his hair. Oh, yeah, now he remembered. Exhaustion. He would have given her the ranch that day if she'd asked for it. And to think he'd actually started to like this woman.

"I wasn't in my right mind when I signed that paper. It will never stand up in a court of law."

"You were tired, not incompetent."

Kati sat on the burgundy leather sofa, one long, bare leg crossed over the other, her chin poking out determinedly. She wore her usual jean shorts and T-shirt, a sight he normally looked forward to after a hot day on the range. But if he kept thinking about her shapely legs and big gray eyes, he might just find himself hog-tied.

Hell's bells, she looked wide-eyed and scared. He was the one who should be scared. Couldn't she see that?

"Look, Kati," he reasoned, spreading his hands wide to show his earnestness. "You're a nice person. You've been great with Evan. I like you, but I don't believe in marriage."

She uncrossed her legs and leaned forward. "This is not about marriage. It's about business. As soon as I have Kati's Angels up and running, I'll be out of your life."

"Why not just let me loan you the money then or cosign your note?" Heck, he'd buy her a business if she'd let him out of this insane agreement. Didn't she understand that marriage took perfectly nice people who liked each other and turned them into arch enemies? He didn't want to be enemies with Kati. He wanted to be… What the heck did he want to be?

He quit pacing long enough to stare at her. Irritably, unreasonably, he wished she'd stop crossing and uncrossing her legs. It was distracting.

She shook her head, and the long silken hair swished around her shoulders. "That would be charity, and I'll never take charity from anyone ever again. The agreement you and I have is a business deal, plain and simple." She stared down at that blasted paper and her hand trembled. "I've kept my part of the deal. Now it's your turn."

Why'd her hands have to shake and make him feel like the biggest heel in Texas? He heaved a ragged sigh and tried a new tack.

"What about Evan? When you get this child-care place of yours up and running, what's going to happen to him?"

Her head popped up. "Have you given up the search?"

"No. Heck, no. I'll never give up, but we have to face the possibility that he may be here awhile."

Colt had reluctantly come to that conclusion not an hour ago while talking to Jace. The lawyer had been very clear that Natosha Parker could have changed her name or even skipped the country by now. If either was the case, the chances of locating her anytime soon were slim to none. She could be found, he'd been assured, but the search could take years.

Colt stomped over to the fireplace and pressed his forehead against the cool oak mantel. He must be getting old. In the past, he'd slithered away from more than one determined woman. Why did escape seem so much more difficult with Kati Winslow?

"What if I refuse?" he asked, turning in time to catch the uncertain expression flitting across her features.

"Would you do that?"

With sagging shoulders, he admitted, "No, I wouldn't." He'd made a commitment, and if he couldn't talk her out of it, he'd be a married man. The notion nearly strangled him.

She slid back onto the couch cushion and recrossed her legs. He willed himself not to watch.

In a last-ditch effort, he went to sit beside her. At this point he was not above begging.

"Don't make me do this, Kati," he said softly, giving her his most beseeching look.

"I have to."

Lost in her kitten eyes, he actually believed her. Was he losing his mind?

Sighing heavily in resignation, he flopped his head back against the couch and said, "You never answered my question about Evan. Don't you care what happens to him once you have your business?"

Kati turned to face him, bringing one knee up to rest on the couch. Her sweet spring scent stirred the air. "I have that all figured out. Evan and I will stay together as long as he needs me. When I move into the center, he'll go with me."

Suddenly forgetting the pleasant pressure of Kati's knee against his, Colt sprang upright, slamming both boots onto the floor. "Evan stays with me."

She blinked in surprise. "I thought you didn't want him."

That was true, wasn't it? He didn't want Evan—or any kid for that matter. Then, why did he have this overwhelming sense of panic at the thought of not seeing the little guy every day?

Pity. That was it. He felt sorry for Evan and didn't want him yanked around like a yo-yo.

"He's my ward, my responsibility. He stays with me."

"Okay, then." She gathered her hair into one hand and pulled the makeshift ponytail over her shoulder, twiddling nervously with the ends. Colt followed the motion, his body responding in the most peculiar way. How could a woman fiddling with her hair be such a turn-on? "I'll drive out every morning to get him and bring him back every night."

"Rattlesnake is forty miles from here."

"Evan is worth the effort."

That seemed to settle the matter. They sat eyeball to eyeball, knee to knee, trying to stare each other down. He blinked first, but not from intimidation.

So she had everything all figured out, did she?

He would be willing to bet she hadn't figured on one teeny aspect. She'd been driving him crazy for weeks. All he could think of was her hair and the way she smelled and the sway of her hips when she walked through the house. Maybe she did it on purpose and maybe she was as innocent as she seemed. At the moment, he didn't give a flying cow chip. He had to make her back down from this crazy agreement.

"Let's get something straight, Kati. I'll keep this nutty agreement if you insist. But we better have us an understanding first. If I have to have a wife, even for a little while, I want a real one."

She swallowed once, twice, her eyes wide. "What do you mean?"

He told her.

She licked her lips and swallowed again.

"If you marry me, you get all of me. A marriage is a marriage." He was startled to discover the idea pleased him as much as it shocked her.

Night after night sitting across from her at the dinner table, standing beside her in the nursery, watching her hair swing behind her as she sashayed through the house. He was going out of his mind living in the same house with her.

A pulse, like a captive quail, fluttered above her collarbone. Colt had the crazy urge to press his mouth against it. Shoot, the notion wasn't any crazier than the rest of this situation.

With a groan of surrender, he closed the gap between them and buried his face in her neck. She tasted every bit as sweet as he'd imagined.

He nibbled his way up her neck and across her jaw until he reached his destination—her lips. Sweet, full, moist lips. He crashed down upon them hungrily—and thought he'd been struck by lightning.

Though her tight little fists relaxed against his chest and she didn't resist, Kati's response was shy and unexpectedly inexperienced. Colt eased back, lightening his kiss. Hadn't anyone ever kissed her this way before? Nudging gently, he parted her lips with his, excited even more by her inexperience. Quivering, she pressed closer. Her breath came in soft pants. Her innocent reaction did nothing for his wavering self-control.

Abruptly, he released her. Another minute of this and he would promise her anything.

"That's the deal, Kati." He rasped. "You. Me. The whole enchilada. Till divorce us do part."

Chapter Five

Thoughts whirling in confusion, Kati lay on her bed, wide-eyed, staring at the ceiling. What had just happened was not in her plans. Not at all. The first time Colt had kissed her all those weeks ago in the nursery had been a fluke, a friendly little peck of gratitude. She'd let it slide without so much as a thought. Well, okay, she'd thought about that kiss a lot, but this thing tonight, holy cow, this was mind numbing.

Colt's insinuation that he expected more from her than a marriage in name only came as a complete shock.

She'd been sure everything would go according to her plan. A marriage of convenience. No commitment, no complications. Just a plain and simple business arrangement. She didn't want to *sleep* with him.

With a groan she dragged the pillow into her lap and pressed it hard against her pulsating body. Who was she kidding? But for her, sex meant emotional commitment, a lowering of the wall she'd long ago built around her heart.

"What am I going to do, Caesar?" she said to the cat sleeping on the dresser. "He expects me to be his real wife." With a bitter smile she added, "Temporarily, of course."

Raising shaky fingers to her lips, she relived the touch of his hot, demanding mouth.

Dear heavens, this wasn't suppose to happen at all. Why, if she wasn't very, very, careful, she'd end up with a baby of her own. The thought of bringing a child into the world to face the same heartache and humiliation she'd suffered was unbearable. She trembled at the idea, resolving to keep a very firm hand on these disturbing feelings for Colt Garret.

"Good grief almighty, Sam, can't you hold that calf's head still for one minute?"

"Sorry, boss." The young cowboy shifted under Colt's thunderous frown, readjusted his grip and pried the struggling calf's mouth open. Other cowboys shot questioning glances at their cranky boss.

Working new calves was always a hot, dirty, tiresome job, but today the June sun seemed hotter and the calves ornerier than ever. Each time the boys ran one through the head gate, Sam was supposed to grab the calf and get the head up and mouth open wide so Colt could shoot a tubeful of medication down its throat. Meanwhile, the cowboys in the back of the chute injected vaccines, checked for malformations, and banded the young bulls.

They had six such chutes working at one time while the rest of the cowboys herded more calves into the corrals. Colt glanced over his shoulder. Already midafternoon and still far too many calves remained to finish today. So many healthy calves should have been good news, but Colt didn't see the good in much of anything today.

Hell's bells, he couldn't get married.

He jabbed the syringe down the hapless calf's throat, releasing the medication. Sam raised the head gate and the calf barreled forward, stumbling and bawling into the feed lot.

Colt removed his hat and swiped a sleeve over his dripping brow.

Dang, it was hot. And he was out of sorts. Ever since Kati had stumbled out of the study last night, flushed and trembling, he'd been in a foul mood. Frustration and guilt had that effect on a man. He hadn't meant to shock her, but she was sexy and sweet, and all this talk of matrimony had him thinking about the only good part of a marriage—the honeymoon.

"Hey, boss, are we gonna work these calves or not?"

Another steer protruded through the head gate, bawling to beat sixty. Five cowboys stood in the dust and muck looking at him with curious expressions.

Trying to erase Kati from his mind, Colt jabbed his hat back on and grabbed hold of a calf. But Kati wouldn't leave him alone. She'd been soft and sweet and innocent. To his dismay, he found the innocence oddly pleasing and enormously exciting.

When he'd first kissed her, he'd hoped to frighten her off, to give her more than she'd bargained for. Trouble was, he got more than he'd bargained for, too.

Good grief almighty, he'd wanted her. Still did. He wanted to bed her all right, but he didn't want to have to marry her to do it.

"Say, Colt, you want me to take over for you here?"

Sam's words yanked Colt back to the cow lot. Kati

Winslow, with her unsophisticated kisses and wild scheme, was interfering with his work.

Viciously he kicked at the metal gate and cursed.

"I'm not worth my wages today, boys." He yanked off his heavy leather gloves and slapped them against his jeans. Dust rose from them, but the smell of cattle and dust couldn't compete with the memory of Kati's flowery scent.

Colt stalked to the corral and called out to one of the men on horseback. A slender young Mexican turned his buckskin and guided him toward the fence where Colt waited.

"Miguel, I've got some things to take care of at the house. I may be a while." He waved his gloves toward the work in progress. "When the boys finish this bunch, let them knock off for an hour or so. It's too blame hot to go at this nonstop."

The foreman nodded his understanding and lifted the reins ready to return to his job. After five years at the Garret Ranch, Miguel was Colt's most valued employee. The quiet foreman worked like a man grateful for the opportunity and never complained about the hours or the heat. The only time he'd ever requested a day off was last week when his wife had a complicated labor and delivery.

"Wait, Miguel."

The young Mexican paused, letting the reins relax.

"How's Juana doing?"

"Not so good." Miguel shook his head. "The new baby is too much for her."

The foreman and his wife had two sons now, the oldest only three. Having come from deep in Mexico, they had no family nearby to help, now that Juana was ill. Miguel, whose devotion to his wife was no secret, worried about her all the time, though he never let personal business interfere with his work.

"Sorry to hear that." Colt wished he knew more about that kind of thing so that he could offer some sage advice. But what did a Garret know about married life? "Take off when the boys do. Go home and check on her."

The foreman and his wife lived in a mobile home on Colt's property, but Miguel would never have left his job without permission. At Colt's words he nodded and flashed a grateful smile.

"She will like that. So will I." He tapped his heels lightly against the horse's flanks and rode back to his work.

Colt watched him ride away. Miguel's was one of the few good marriages he'd ever witnessed, and with a twinge of regret, he knew no Garret would ever understand that kind of commitment. He had to make Kati see that once and for all.

Colt jogged to his truck and headed to the house.

He found her in the kitchen with Cookie. Her back was to him so that he noted the long French braid hanging to her waist and the smooth expanse of leg running from her shorts to her bare feet. He was more than a little irked that she'd braided her hair when he preferred it long and loose. The thought pulled him up short, and he stopped in the doorway, lounging there until she noticed him. Since when had he started paying that much attention to a woman's hair?

Cookie noticed him first.

"Hey, boss, what are you doing up here this time of day?"

"Came to talk to Kati."

He tried to say the words casually, but the moment he spoke, Kati froze. She didn't turn around. She simply stood where she was as still as a statue, a faint pink tinge creeping up the back of her neck. Guilt knifed through Colt and he wanted to go to her and apologize for scaring her, for embarrassing her. Heck, for whatever it was he'd done.

Curiously Cookie looked back and forth between the two of them. "Go ahead, Miss Kati. I'll finish that up."

She hesitated, taking an inordinate amount of time to wash and dry her hands. When she finally turned, she wouldn't look at him. Her face was flushed, and she licked her lips in that nervous manner that both angered and stirred him.

Eyes averted, chin in the air, she marched out of the kitchen and down the hall toward his study. He followed, hating himself for relishing the sway of her braid—and her bottom.

Kati wished to goodness Colt would stop staring at her like he was a coyote and she a rabbit. Facing him was hard enough after she'd acted a fool over him last night.

Once they stepped inside the study and closed the door—an action that sent her pulse up a notch—Colt leaned his lanky form against the fireplace, folded his arms and stared.

She fidgeted self-consciously and licked her suddenly dry lips. Colt followed the action. A bright gleam leaped into his eyes.

"You're interfering with my work."

He broke from the fireplace and stalked toward her, all power and heat and dusty leather. An eyelash away, he paused, frowning uncertainly. Then with a groan he yanked her to him, his lips capturing hers. Kati's plan for dignified resistance disappeared. She melted against him, braced for an onslaught of passion, for a hungry, devouring mouth to match the rapacious gleam in his eyes. Instead, he destroyed her will completely with his tenderness. He held her like delicate crystal, his rough cowboy hands caressing her back, his lips pleading for mercy. Kati's traitorous heart responded wildly. Blood rushed to her head.

"Colt, please," she begged when he moved his mouth to her neck, though whether she begged for more or for mercy, she couldn't say. His warm breath panted against her throat before he dropped his arms and stepped away. Kati reeled backward and wilted weakly onto the sofa.

"I didn't come up here to do that," he said shortly.

"Then why did you?" She pressed trembling hands to her hot cheeks.

"This whole talk of marriage has made me loco. And last night…" He shook his head, then pointed a finger in her direction. "You have to understand something, Kati. I'm a man, not some pansy who can be married to a beautiful, sexy woman without wanting her."

He paced the burgundy carpet ranting about the ridiculous situation she'd put them into, but Kati didn't hear another word. She'd stopped listening the minute he said *beautiful* and *sexy*. Not that she believed such a thing, but, oh, the words did sound so nice just this once.

Her thoughts flew away to the long-ago fantasy of a loving husband and family, but she quickly reined them in. Hadn't she vowed to leave fantasy behind? To face reality? There would be no loving man, no family to cherish. Not for Kati Winslow. Some women just weren't meant for love, and she was one of them. Colt was a normal man who wanted to sleep with her, but he made no pretense about love. Love was a fantasy, a dream for other people. She was far too smart and experienced to think otherwise.

Her only dreams were the ones she could accomplish on her own. Sadly, fulfilling those dreams meant forcing Colt into a situation he despised, but she had to do it. After all, their marriage would only be temporary. Then he could return to his life and forget all about her. And she could do the same. No harm, no foul.

"Colt."

"What?" he said, turning to face her.

"I made some wedding plans today."

He shoved both hands through his hair, his mouth open in disbelief. "You haven't heard a word I've said, have you?"

"No." Well, not since the beautiful and sexy part, anyway.

With a resigned sigh, he flopped into a chair and slouched down. His boots left traces of dust along the carpet.

"We're getting married Saturday afternoon."

Colt jerked. His throat bobbed twice. "Saturday's only three days away."

"Right. We'll—" Her voice wobbled. She cleared her throat and started again. "We'll marry on Saturday, start the loan proceedings on Monday, and in six months, maximum, you'll be jetting off to Reno for a divorce."

"Nope." Colt shook his head. "Not Reno. My attorney says they don't have quickie divorces in Nevada anymore."

"Well then, I'll agree to a Texas divorce."

"Takes too long. And Jace says Texas divorce courts can get real sticky."

Confusion twisted inside her. "Then I don't know what to do."

"We can forget the whole crazy idea."

"I can't."

"All right, then, if you insist on going through with this thing." He heaved a ragged sigh. "According to Jace, a trip down to the Dominican Republic is the easiest way out. A fast and relatively painless way to dissolve an unwanted marriage."

Marriage and divorce in the same conversation. The notion was painful even for Kati, who knew she'd never find a love of her own. Her chest ached miserably. Even a pretend marriage deserved better. Especially marriage to a man like Colt Garret.

Chapter Six

"Colt, you old sidewinder, where are you?"

Colt sat in his office preparing the weekly payroll. At the sound of a rich male voice calling his name he slammed the ledger and groaned. Caesar, lying inches away, awoke with a start and leaped down from the desk wearing an injured look. Colt thought things were bad already, but they'd just gotten worse. Jett was home.

The study door slammed backward, vibrating on its hinges. Jett strode into the room grinning as if he'd just won the all-round cowboy title at the National Finals Rodeo. That was the way Jett always appeared. Breezing in and out with a smile and a few wild stories.

Times like now when the ranch was so busy and the responsibilities so heavy, Colt envied his brother's free-wheeling lifestyle. Jett had the easy part—though that had been the deal between them years ago. Colt retained controlling interest and ran things his way. Jett shared expenses and profits without questioning Colt's decisions.

Colt rose from his desk, striding across the room to wrap his brother in a bear hug, acknowledging deep down that he wouldn't trade places with him for anything. He'd grown roots and Jett hadn't.

"What tornado blew you in?" Colt stepped back to survey his baby brother.

Jett was a good-looking cuss just like all the Garret men. Though not as tall as Colt, Jett shared his dark features, right down to the tiny sun lines around his eyes. In Jett's case they were undoubtedly laugh lines.

Jett proved as much by laughing at his brother's question. "I got bunged-up some at the rodeo over in Odessa a couple of nights ago. Figured home was as good a place as any to rest up a bit."

Colt now saw what he hadn't noticed before. Jett held his right arm at an odd angle against his body. "What have you done this time, boy?"

"Ah, dislocated my shoulder. Got hung up on a pretty rank bull that liked to buck. Nothing serious, but it's got me on the sidelines for a few days."

Having done some rodeoing himself, Colt knew the awful feeling of getting "hung up." With the right hand securely tied during the eight-second ride, it was a minor miracle that every cowboy didn't lose an arm when he jumped from the bull's back. Occasionally the rope didn't release and the cowboy's body hung by that one hand, flopping like a rag doll until the bullfighters could set him free. Getting hung up was one of the reasons he was a rancher now instead of a bull rider.

"Too bad you're wounded, Jett," he grinned, knowing his brother wore his injuries like a badge of honor. "We could sure use some help around here."

Jett laughed. "Give me a couple of days, and I'll be out of your hair."

"That's what I figured." Ranching was never Jett's idea of a good time.

The brothers stood grinning at each other until something caught Jett's eye.

"What is that?" He pointed at a blue baby rattle and started toward it slowly. He picked the toy up from the chair and held it toward Colt. "Is this what I think it is?"

Colt's troubles all came back to him. He propped a hip on the corner of his desk and answered tiredly, "You've been gone awhile."

"Not that long."

"Sit down, Jett. I need your help."

"Oh, no." Turning the rattle over and over in his hands, a look of horror on his face, Jett eased himself into a chair. "Brother, what have you done?"

Colt rubbed at the tension in his neck. "I don't even know where to begin."

"You're scaring me, man." Jett took off his hat and plastered it against his chest. "You're scaring me real bad."

Unsure how to break the news, Colt reached inside his desk and removed a copy of Evan's custody papers and the letter that had arrived with them. He handed them to his wary brother.

Jett's face turned serious as he scanned the information. "Is this some woman you knew?"

"Not that I know of."

"So the baby's not yours?"

"Not you, too." At Jett's questioning look, Colt explained, "Everyone keeps asking me that."

"Well?"

"Well, what?" That question was starting to wear thin. Jett of all people should know better. "No, Evan is not my son. Not naturally, anyway, but I'm trying to do right by him."

Jett raised an eyebrow. "Getting attached, are you?"

"No!" he yelled, then on second thought admitted, "Maybe." He paced to the window and back. "I'm trying to find this Natosha woman, but she's disappeared without a trace."

"That's not good. How can a single cowboy who has nearly as many women after him as his baby brother does—" Jett paused to grin at his own humor "—take care of a baby?"

"That's where things start getting complicated." He flopped down at the desk, folding his hands as if in prayer and told Jett about Kati.

Throughout the story, Jett's expression grew more and more incredulous until he was nearly levitating above his chair.

"Have you lost your mind?" Jett shouted when the story ended.

"That has occurred to me."

"You don't actually want to marry this woman, do you?"

Colt's mouth opened and shut twice before he was able to answer. Jett was the one losing his mind if he thought for one minute Colt wanted to get married. He didn't. Did he?

"Of course not. We both know what marriage does to people."

"Thank goodness." Jett stood and slapped his brother's shoulder. "You had me scared there for a minute. I thought you were actually going to go through with this thing."

"I am."

"What?" Jett threw up both hands. "Whoa. Wait a minute. Hold on. You don't want to marry her but you're going to?"

"Temporarily."

Jett bared his teeth and hissed. "Why do I hate the sound of this?"

Colt explained the dilemma again, emphasizing the quickie divorce part. Clearly stated, the plan actually didn't sound as horrible as he'd thought. Jett, on the other hand, having lived through the same nightmare of broken homes that Colt had, saw the situation differently.

"Back out now. Once she gets her hooks into you and this ranch, she'll never let go." Jett was pacing the carpet. "This is a trap, brother. I can smell it like a 'coon dog smells a 'possum."

"A man's only as good as his word. You know I won't back down from a promise." Colt applied a thumb and index finger to his eye sockets, rubbing hard, then exhaled loudly. "The only way to stop the thing is if Kati changes her mind. And I'm working on that."

Jett stopped dead still in front of the desk. "How?"

Slowly, Colt brought his gaze on a level with Jett's. "By putting on a little pressure to scare her off."

"I don't get it."

"Sure you do." He shifted uncomfortably. "She wants a marriage in name only. I *didn't* promise her that."

Funny, he suddenly didn't want to discuss this aspect of his relationship with Kati. Not even with Jett.

"Come on," Jett responded with disbelief. "We Garret brothers aren't exactly the ugliest guys around. Why would any woman want a loveless marriage when they could have one of us to snuggle up with?'' Jett raised his eyebrows into question marks. ''Unless she's gay…or ugly as sin.''

Now, why did Jett have to say that? He didn't even know Kati. Sure, he and his brother had talked man talk about dozens of women over the years, but discussing Kati that way seemed wrong somehow. After all, she could end up being his wife in a day or two. He blanched at the thought but still felt a need to defend Kati.

''That sort of thing makes her nervous. She's kind of inexperienced.''

Jett guffawed. ''I think you're falling for the oldest trick in the book. I've met my share of women and they're all experienced, Colt. Sometimes they just hold out for a better deal. Like this ranch. You're not exactly broke, you know, and from what you tell me, this Kati woman doesn't have anything.''

''Maybe you've been meeting the wrong women,'' Colt growled, surprised by the intensity of his anger. He'd been around plenty of experienced, conniving women, and Kati didn't fit the mold.

''Maybe you found one that's playing you like a bass fiddle.''

Jett hadn't been home an hour and already he was getting on Colt's nerves. Usually they were two peas in a pod, but if Jett opened his fat mouth once more about Kati, Colt just might have to shut it for him.

In confusion, Colt scrubbed angrily at his face and threw his head back, staring up at the circling ceiling fan. The whirring noise set his teeth on edge.

Caesar chose that moment to ease out from under the desk to sniff Jett's boots.

''What the devil is this?''

Colt sighed. "Kati's cat."

"You hate cats."

"Yeah, but I can't convince him of that."

"Babies, nannies, cats. Now I know you're losing it."

"Look, Jett, I need your help here, not your snide remarks. Two days from now, barring a miracle, I'm going to be a married man. Either make a useful suggestion or shut up."

"You want a useful suggestion?" With his thumb, Jett pushed at the brim of his hat and grinned. "I'll give you two. Either toss this Kati Winslow out while you can, cat and all, or get your good suit cleaned."

Saturday. D-Day. Colt sat at his desk, certain the top of his head would blow off before four o'clock. The past two days had flown by in a flurry of blood tests, license and praying for the miracle that hadn't come. He'd done everything he could to dissuade Kati from going through with this thing, but he'd failed miserably. The more he skulked around like some pervert, muttering about a real marriage, the more determined she became.

This morning at breakfast, she'd been pale as a ghost and just as quiet. He could relate to the terror in her eyes. He felt the same way for different reasons. At least, he supposed they were different.

Bracing his forehead on the desktop, he covered his head with his hands. How had he come to make so many bad decisions in such a short span of time? In one month his entire world had turned upside down.

Even Jett, his own flesh-and-blood brother, had abandoned him in his time of need. Not that he thought Colt should get married. Not by a long shot. But, after he'd met Kati and hung around her awhile, he'd shrugged his shoulder and agreed that Colt had his butt in a bind. A lot of help he was.

And Cookie sided with Kati, making noises about worthless cowboys who couldn't keep their hands to themselves, sure that Colt must have compromised her virtue. Maybe he would feel better if he had.

"Colt."

He jumped as if he'd been shot. Heck, he wished somebody *would* shoot him and put him out of his misery.

Even with his forehead pressed against the desktop, he knew his visitor was Kati. No other voice slid across his name like warm honey.

Slowly he raised his head. She smiled, and he felt as if the sun had come out after two days of rain.

"What?" he asked, not sounding nearly as grouchy as he'd felt a moment ago.

She pointed. "You have a crease on your forehead."

"Oh." His hand went to the spot. "The desk."

"Yes." She came around the desk, high heels swishing over the carpet to stand beside his chair. "Here."

When he raised his eyes in question, she smiled again and touched his forehead, massaging the wrinkled skin. Her fingers trembled as she moved closer.

Colt's stomach lifted. Her breasts were not six inches from his face. He could see them rise and fall with each breath she took, and could smell the mix of flowers and baby powder that clung to her all the time. The combination was highly erotic to a man who'd lain awake last night wondering if he would be sharing a bed with this woman tonight.

"There." She dropped her hand and stepped back,

straightening her shoulders. "That's better. Are you ready?"

"It's not too late to call the whole thing off."

"Cookie agreed to watch Evan while we run into town. We won't be long."

"Kati." He grabbed her hand. Her skin was ice-cold. "We're not going after ice cream."

Her gray eyes grew large as she whispered, "I know that."

Carefully she withdrew her hand and gathered a small white purse from the desktop. Squaring her shoulders, she took a deep breath and walked determinedly to the door.

Already straining at the ring in his nose, Colt followed her out to the truck.

The drive to town was mostly silent. Colt fiddled with the radio a bit, but none of the stations suited him. He gave up and slid a CD into the player.

"Do you like George Strait?"

Such a stupid question. He was going to marry her, and he didn't even know if she liked country music.

At her nod, he adjusted the volume and settled into the drive, his hands strangling the steering wheel.

Kati could hardly take her eyes off him. They'd not discussed what to wear today, and she wouldn't have been surprised if he'd worn work clothes. But he hadn't. He looked resplendent in a black Western-cut jacket, black jeans, hat, boots, and string tie with a crisp white shirt contrasting against his sun-darkened face. This gorgeous cowboy was enough to take any woman's breath away, and he'd actually agreed to be her husband. At least for a while.

She gazed down at her dress, the simple yellow

sheath she'd bought for Easter. A short jacket with white embroidered daisies dressed the outfit up a bit, and she'd worn her only pair of white heels. Still, she knew how the peahen must feel beside her more glorious mate.

Kati's heart swelled with a bizarre sense of joy. Colt Garret was not only a gorgeous cowboy, he was an honorable man. He could have refused to go through with this, and she could have done nothing. But he hadn't. As much as he hated the idea of marriage, he'd dressed up in his Sunday clothes to keep his promise.

The muscles in Colt's leg flexed as he slowed for a hay baler crossing the road. His work-honed body fascinated her. She loved looking at him, touching him, and the notion frightened her. Would he really demand his rights as a husband? If he did, could she refuse? Would she want to?

Her nerves tightened at the prospect. She had to. If she gave herself to Colt, she'd be lost forever. The pain of loving him, then losing him, would be too much to bear. She had made a promise, too, and she would keep her end of the bargain.

With steely control she redirected her gaze, riding the rest of the way into town with her attention glued to the golden plains of Texas and the pure country sound of a steel guitar.

Heat rose from the sidewalk in waves as Kati and Colt made their way into the low-slung brick building marked County Courthouse. Inside the cool, fluorescent-lit hallway Colt paused. ''You sure about this, Kati?''

The butterflies in her stomach fluttered wildly. ''No, but I have to.''

He shook his head slowly in exasperation. "Temporary. This is only temporary."

"Absolutely." Like everything else, she wanted to say.

He took her elbow and guided her over the white industrial tile and through a glass door marked Judge Carson. Her heels tapped out a hollow echo in the quiet building, but she was certain her heart pounded louder.

For Kati, the next minutes passed in a blur. She and Colt stood side by side in front of a surprisingly youthful judge who read from a small maroon book. The words sailed over her head like lost helium balloons. She was far too busy trying to stand up to listen. Her knees wobbled and her ears rang. Once she even thought she might faint. Colt must have thought so, too, because he looked at her in concern and slid an arm around her waist. He was rock hard and solid, giving her some of his strength, though a tremor ran through him from time to time.

"Do you have the ring?" the judge asked.

"Oh, no," she whispered. "I forgot about the ring."

Colt returned her horrified look with one of his own. "So did I." Then his expression lightened. "Does that mean we can't get married?"

"No, no, not at all," the judge assured them. "You can add the ring later. It's not a necessity. We'll continue without it."

Though Colt looked crestfallen, the ceremony continued, and in less time than he could say, "Hog-tied," the judge pronounced them man and wife.

"You may kiss your bride, Mr. Garret," the judge said with a smile.

Colt turned her in his arms and stared down at her,

an odd light in his eyes. His lips curved the tiniest bit before he bent his head and pressed his mouth softly against hers.

"You're as white as a sheet," Colt told her as they settled into the pickup ready for the long drive home.

"So are you."

He glanced up into the mirror. "I am not. I'm steady as a rock." He stuck a hand out to prove it, then grinned wryly and slammed his hand down on the steering wheel when his fingers made a liar out of him.

Kati drew in a deep shuddering breath and slithered down into the seat. "At least it's over."

"Yeah. It's over," he repeated. Suddenly he stiffened and fiercely gripped the steering wheel. "Good grief almighty, I'm a married man."

"Temporarily," she reminded him in a faint voice.

He exhaled in relief. "Right. It's only temporary." Then why did he feel this overwhelming sense of exhilaration as though he'd won the Texas lottery? He'd expected to feel depressed, not exhilarated.

He sneaked a look at Kati, her gray eyes huge in a pale face, and longed to comfort her. Stupid reaction, he knew, but there it was, big as Dallas. "Scoot over here," he said gruffly.

"Excuse me?"

He patted the seat beside him. "You're my wife now. You have to sit by me. It's a rule."

"A rule." She said it doubtfully, but a ghost of a smile tickled her lips. "Why haven't I ever heard of this rule before?"

"Because you, pretty lady, have never been married before." Grasping her wrist, he gave a gentle tug. "Come on. Scoot. The bankers may be watching."

Kati shot a furtive glance out the side window, an

action that made Colt want to laugh. Propelled into action, Kati slid across the long bench seat, her pretty yellow dress easing upward as she came. Swallowing hard, Colt forced his gaze from the sight of her long, smooth legs, though his brain wouldn't stop wondering if she was wearing panty hose.

During the forty-mile drive, Colt called himself ten kinds of idiot. Having Kati beside him, her clean scent driving him crazy and the pressure of her warm thigh against his, tormented his already strained libido. To make matters worse, she was funny and sweet and laughed at every corny joke he told. A man could get used to a woman like that, and Kati clearly wasn't interested in a real marriage any more than he was. And he wasn't. He couldn't be.

Inside forty-five minutes, the truck, spewing dust and gravel, barreled beneath the cross timbers of Garret Ranch. A bay horse whinnied and galloped alongside white metal fencing, racing the truck down the long driveway.

Colt was so busy enjoying the pleasure on Kati's face as she watched the horse, his mane and tail flying, that he didn't notice the activity around the ranch house until the truck ground to a halt.

"What in blazes is going on?" Killing the motor, Colt frowned at the dozen or so trucks and cars parked on the sparse green lawn.

Kati unsnapped her seat belt and blinked in bewilderment. "Looks like someone decided to have a party while we were gone."

They both froze, eyes meeting in stunned comprehension.

"You don't think Cookie…?" Recognizing the vehicles of ranch hands and neighbors, the suspicion in Colt's gut increased. Dadblast that old geezer. What had he done?

"Surely he didn't." Kati gripped the dash. "We told him this wasn't a real marriage."

"Did he mention a wedding cake to you?"

"Well, yes, sort of." If such a thing was possible, Kati looked more horrified than he felt.

"Oh, boy." Briefly Colt laid his head on the steering wheel. Then, in defeat, he took Kati's soft hand in his. "Come on, Mrs. Garret. Whether we like it or not, looks like we have a wedding reception to attend."

As soon as they walked through the door, a hoard of well-wishers surrounded them. Tightness banded Kati's chest. Dear sweet old Cookie, convinced she was the perfect mate for his boss, was determined to celebrate. Kati felt like such a hypocrite.

While they'd been gone, someone—Cookie and the few women on the ranch, she would later discover— had decorated the living room with richly scented yellow roses and crepe paper wedding bells. A long table stretched across one end of the massive room, a three-layer wedding cake dabbed with more yellow roses perched in the center. Around the cake were enough bottles of champagne to wipe out half the Texas Panhandle, and from somewhere came the predictable strains of the "Yellow Rose of Texas." Everything was perfect. Everything except the marriage itself. Kati's heart ached, both with joy that someone even cared and with sadness that these nice people were celebrating a charade.

Cookie was in his element. He sashayed around, giving orders, taking pictures, toting Evan on one hip like a plump grandma. Knowing Cookie, he'd put one of those pictures in the local newspapers, along with an announcement of the nuptials.

With a guilty sigh, she acknowledged one benefit of this reception. Word of their marriage would get back to town, convincing the necessary parties that it was the real deal.

At one point, the sweet old cook whipped across the room carrying a rose.

With a glare at Colt, he pressed the rose into Kati's hand, grumbling. ''Ignorant cowpoke didn't have sense enough to buy you no flowers. Even an old sailor knows better than that. What are you gonna throw to the ladies without a bouquet?''

''Cookie, I'm not throwing the bouquet. I told you—''

Cookie waved a flabby arm. ''I don't want to hear it. This is your weddin' day, and you're sure enough going to toss that flower.''

When she looked to Colt for help, he shrugged and said, ''Humor him, Kati. You can't win when he gets like this.''

''But I really should tend to Evan.'' She reached for the child only to have Cookie draw back.

''You ain't taking this boy. Why, every woman in this place is dying to get their hands on him. He's a perfect lady magnet for an old salt like me.'' With a delighted chortle, he whipped away before Kati could argue.

''Let him go.'' Colt took her elbow and pulled her aside, his darkly handsome face serious. ''I haven't seen Cookie havin' this much fun since his fiancée died.''

Kati's insides lurched as she watched the cook head

straight toward an attractive older woman. "Cookie was engaged?"

"About fifteen years ago. She died in a car wreck a couple of weeks before the wedding." His gaze followed the portly cook. "Even if this party isn't real, he believes it is. Let him have his fun, okay?"

Kati gripped the rose to her heart. "Of course I will. Poor, sweet old Cookie. I had no idea."

"The rest of these yahoos think it's real, too, so we might as well go along for the ride. Anything less, they'll be embarrassed and so will we. And word will fly back to town so fast your loan will be denied before you can say 'collateral.'"

Standing this close to Colt, looking into his dark brown eyes and remembering that he was actually her husband—for now—moved the loan to the back burner of her brain. And when he touched her with those tender-tough hands, she didn't even remember her name much less her ambition.

"Hey, bro." Jett's voice interrupted them as he sauntered toward them. "Don't I get to kiss the bride?"

Before either Kati or Colt could react to such an outlandish request, Jett swept Kati into his arms and kissed her. His mouth was warm and smiling and brotherly, nothing at all like Colt's, but when he lifted his face and laughed down at her, Kati blushed from head to toe.

Yanking her away, Colt hooked an arm around her waist and snugged her close to his side. "Go find your own woman, *bro.*"

There was something fierce and possessive in Colt's manner—something so real that Jett backed off and threw up his hands. "What's the matter, bro? Afraid she'll like my kisses better than yours?" He grinned his crooked grin at Kati. "Look out, Kati. You've married you one jealous cowboy."

"Don't you have a rodeo to go to?" Colt asked.

Jett laughed at the scowl on his brother's face. "What? And miss all the excitement around here? I haven't had so much fun since that college kid had a runaway on your stud horse."

"This isn't funny, Jett."

"Depends on your perspective, I guess. Now, if you'll excuse me, Mr. Married Man, I think I see a gorgeous single female giving me the eye." With a quirky pump of his black brows, he sauntered away.

"He was only teasing," Kati said as a frowning Colt took her hand and led her toward the refreshment table. "Are you angry?"

"That he kissed you?" He handed her a flute of champagne. "No, darlin', not with you anyway. My baby brother has a way of making a nuisance of himself, but if anybody's gonna kiss you," he growled down at her with a wink, "it's gonna be me."

Kati nearly choked on the tart drink. Resisting this devastating attraction to Colt strained her willpower to the shattering point. Adding inhibition-lowering champagne to an already lethal mix of a sentimental wedding reception and a sexy, charming husband might not be the wisest idea, but she took a long sip to ease her tension just the same.

As the reception moved into full swing, Colt guided her among his friends and employees, the smile on his lips as tight as the arm around Kati's waist. He was as charming as sin, pulling off the charade as easily as he rode a horse. Kati, on the other hand, felt as stiff as starched underwear.

Somehow they survived the evening. At Cookie's insistence, Kati tossed the bouquet. Then she and Colt cut the cake and managed to look surprisingly happy doing it. Colt whispered something silly in her ear, and she found herself laughing. And when some of the rowdier cowboys demanded that Colt kiss the bride, he wrapped her in a bear hug and kissed her breathless. The crowd was delighted, of course, while Kati trembled with trepidation. The wine, the kiss and the man were all potent intoxicants that she could not succumb to.

At last the guests began to dwindle, and though Kati had been happy to spend time with the other women, especially the shyly smiling Juana Rodriguez, she was glad to see them go. When there were only a few cowboys, including Colt, leaning on the fireplace telling lies, Kati managed to slip away.

After a long, soothing bath, she donned an oversize T-shirt and plopped onto the bed for a moment's rest. Soon she'd have to wrestle Evan from Cookie and get him settled for the night, but right now she needed to catch her breath and calm her overwrought nerves. Getting married had been strange enough, but coming home to a reception had been—sweet, actually. Uncomfortable as all get-out under the circumstances, but very sweet indeed. Colt had behaved almost loverlike, especially after Jett had kissed her. Funny how the brothers looked so much alike but kissed so differently. Kati raised her fingertips to her lips, the memory of Colt's kisses far stronger than that of Jett's.

As she closed her eyes, reliving Colt's cake-tinged kiss, the bedroom door clicked open. "Come on in, Cookie," she said without looking up, certain Cookie was bringing the baby to her. "I'm sure he's ready for bed."

The springs groaned and the bed sank to one side. A warm woodsy scent drifted into Kati's consciousness.

"He *is* ready for bed." Colt's rich baritone hinted that he wasn't talking about Evan.

So much for soothing her frayed nerves. Every one of them stood at attention. Her heart rate went from normal to tachycardia in 0.2 seconds.

"Evan," she protested, wishing like crazy she had on more clothes. "I have to see to Evan."

"He's gone." At her wide-eyed look, he continued. "Cookie and Jett took him to Jett's camper for the night."

Cookie and Jett were gone, too. She and Colt were alone in this enormous house. Her pulses tap-danced against her skin. Alone with Colt, the sexiest, most masculine man on earth, who also happened to be her husband.

In the butter-cream light shafting in from the bathroom, Kati saw that her bridegroom had shed his coat and tie and boots. His shirt hung open so that Kati glimpsed the wide, tanned chest sprinkled with dark hairs. Her gaze traveled downward to his rippling belly and the vee of fine hairs above his waistband.

She swallowed a knot as yearning turned to desire. This wasn't going to be easy. Not easy at all. "It's been a long, nerve-racking day, Colt."

"I'm your husband now, Kati."

"Only on paper." Tugging at the far too short T-shirt, she squeezed her eyes shut. If she dared look at him, all gorgeous and dark and lustful, she might not have the strength to keep this a marriage in name only. She might not want to.

When he touched her arm, her eyes flew open again.

He was still there, her brand-new husband, looking good enough to eat for dessert.

"I never agreed to a marriage in name only." His soft, seductive voice slid over her sensitive nerve endings. "Sleeping apart doesn't make sense. We've got the official piece of paper, so why not enjoy the only good thing about marriage?"

Didn't he understand the complications of sex? So what if she wanted him. She'd wanted a lot of things in her life that she couldn't have. Self-preservation was far more important than self-indulgence. She'd come here with one purpose in mind, but for the life of her she couldn't remember what that purpose was when Colt looked at her this way.

"I want you, Kati." His hand slid over her arm lightly, blazing a trail of goose bumps. "Don't you want me?"

"I can't. Please understand."

"Why? I'm a man. You're a woman. And we *are* married." He leaned closer, his chest grazing hers.

"But not for long." She swallowed hard, an action that drew Colt's attention to her throat. He traced the hollow of her throat with one finger. Almost moaning, Kati clamped her eyes closed and shivered in response, her words forced. "I haven't— I'm not— I don't believe in affairs."

"How could it be an affair when we're married? Unless you're not attracted to me." He seemed sincere, as though he doubted his potent effect on her. "Is that the problem?"

Grasping the lifeline, Kati replied, "Yes, that's it."

Colt's hand stilled. Her tattletale pulse pecked against his callused fingers. "It is?"

"Yes," she choked.

"Are you saying my kisses don't affect you?"

"Yes." Liar, liar, pants on fire. Boy, was that a true saying if there ever was one.

"Then you won't mind if I…"

In the next heartbeat Colt's lips closed over hers and she was lost, melting into the warmth and pleasure of his champagne mouth and tongue joined to hers. Sensations she'd sublimated for so long erupted with the violent force of Mount Saint Helens.

When the delicious pressure of Colt's mouth suddenly disappeared, disappointment replaced it. Drat her traitorous heart. Why had she married a man she'd once had a crush on?

Hot from head to toe, Kati dared to peek at her husband. Oh dear, he was undressing and sliding into bed beside her, wearing only a pair of boxers that didn't hide the fact that he wanted his new wife in the worst way. Kati sat bolt upright and clutched the neck of her T-shirt. "What…what are you doing?"

"Sleeping with my wife. If you're not attracted to me, then what difference does it make? I can kiss you and hold you and you won't get turned on, so there's no need to worry about your virtue. Right?"

Why did that sound off-kilter? Fuzzy-headed from Colt's devastating kiss and too much champagne, Kati couldn't think straight to save her liver.

"I don't want to…to—" She couldn't get the words out.

"Make love?" His husky voice was amused.

"Right."

"I do." At her sharp intake of breath, he relented. "But I won't. Not unless you want to. But if I have to be a married man, I am *not* sleeping alone. At least give me that."

"No, this is crazy. I won't." But she stayed in the bed, aware of his washboard belly touching her upper thighs.

"We can sleep here or in my bed or on the kitchen floor for all I care, but wherever you choose, we're sleeping together," he insisted. "You're getting what you want out of this crazy marriage of ours, so at least give me the courtesy of behaving like a real wife. I won't have every hand on this ranch thinking I'm an idiot. A man has his pride, you know."

Kati gnawed on her lip as she stared into the nuclear gaze of her make-believe husband. She'd never considered his point of view before. Naturally, he'd be embarrassed for others to know he'd made a marriage of convenience with the nanny. Just look at the way Jett had teased him. Considering all Colt was giving her, maybe she could do this one thing for him.

"Okay," she relented, wondering how on earth she would be able to lie beside him every night without going out of her mind. "You can sleep in here at night, and I'll pretend to be your wife during the day. But that's all. No hanky-panky."

"Spoilsport," he muttered with a wry grin that made her stomach quiver. "Okay, if you insist, no hanky-panky. But a real wife kisses her husband." He reached for her braid and tugged, drawing her down beside him. "And holds him…" He placed her arms around his neck.

When his mouth found hers again, she gave herself fully to the kiss, knowing moments like these were unfailingly temporary. Heat sizzled past her lips, flowing down her body to form a molten pit low in her belly. Desire more potent than anything she'd ever experienced threatened to burn her alive. She didn't want the kiss to end. Ever. Pressing closer and closer to Colt's hard, hungry body, she longed to melt into him, to be part of him. Any minute now she was certain her body would spontaneously combust.

When Colt suddenly ended the glorious exploration of her mouth and pulled her into the spoon of his body, Kati couldn't believe the degree of disappointment. As she lay breathless, struggling to stop the fierce craving of her body, Colt's hot, sexy voice whispered against her ear.

"It's a good thing we're not attracted to each other."

Chapter Seven

Calves bawled and mother cows answered. Cowboys milled around on horseback, hollering orders and telling weekend stories. Colt slammed the door of his four-wheel-drive and looked across the pasture, squinting against the morning sun. He was tired, and the day had only started a couple of hours ago. Heck, he was exhausted. How could he sleep with his libido in high gear and a sexy woman curled beside him in bed? He'd cursed himself for a fool a thousand times for insisting on sleeping with her, but every time he started toward his own bedroom, the lure of her soft, round body curving into his drew him right back. Somewhere he'd lost his mind, and for the life of him, he couldn't find it.

At first he'd thought he was sleeping with her to prove a point, to save face, but the fact of the business was, he just plain wanted to be near Kati. If he could keep his hands off her, the situation wouldn't be so bad, but he couldn't do that either. Craziest mess he'd ever gotten into.

"Hey, boss, how do you like being a married man?" a rangy cowboy called from horseback.

If they only knew, he'd be the laughingstock of the barnyard. Colt shot a cranky look that brought hoots of laughter from the others nearby. One of them began singing a song about a ball and chain, his off-key tenor sending his buddies into near hysteria.

"I think Colt needs a week off to recover from the honeymoon. Looks pretty tired to me."

With a scowl, Colt started pulling fence posts from the back of the truck.

They were right about one thing. He needed a week to recover from waking up next to Kati. Rolling out of the bed and leaving her with only a kiss on the forehead wasn't easy. This morning she'd been snuggled against him, her hair all tangled around his hands and face so that he was captured. It was his own fault. She braided her hair before bed, but he took it down as soon as he'd crawled in beside her.

He couldn't figure out what was going on. Even now, just thinking about her, he wanted to throw down his fencing pliers and go back to the house. He'd had other women, plenty of them, but since Kati entered his life he'd been able to think of little else. That wasn't like him. Normally he would have a fling, then go on back to business as usual. Maybe that was the problem. He hadn't actually *had* Kati, and the chase had always been more fun that the catch.

Or maybe he was attracted by the novelty of her inexperience, her shy behavior when they were alone. Despite her earlier protests she seemed to welcome his kisses, and that gave him hope that she'd eventually welcome the rest of him. Maybe she really was innocent and needed this time to be wooed. He enjoyed that notion. A man liked to think he was the only one who'd ever touched his woman whether it was true or not.

Yanking the hat from his head, he rubbed wearily at his perspiring temples. What was wrong with him? Kati wasn't his woman, and he had no right to teach her things that a real husband should teach her someday. No matter that she was his wife all signed and legal. She wasn't really his and that wasn't about to change. A special lady like Kati deserved a man who could give her a happy life. He hated the way his gut twisted every time he thought of Kati in some other man's arms, but she deserved an honorable man committed to her happiness. And there wasn't a Garret alive who even understood the word *commitment.*

"Looks like she's had all of you she wanted already, bro." Jett leaned lazily against the truck fender, chewing a piece of grass.

"What are you talking about?" Colt spun in the direction of Jett's hitched chin. When his brother grinned, Colt wanted to knock his head off.

In the distance a plume of dust spiraled upward like a dust devil. Kati's green compact spun down the driveway.

Late that afternoon an exhilarated Kati returned from town. After settling a tired, fussy Evan for a nap, she spread the papers on Colt's desk eager to show him all she'd accomplished. He would be so pleased to know she'd kept her promise. Truth was, she had to get on with the plan. Sleeping next to Colt's work-honed body was killing her.

Despite her desperate need for self-preservation, she'd wanted him to kiss her and hold her. She knew she shouldn't, but she couldn't help herself. More than once she'd awakened to find his hands in places they shouldn't be, and she'd used every ounce of her resolve not to turn in his arms and give him all her love. For some reason Colt Garret, the man who endangered her heart, wanted to play house, and for this little while, Kati drifted with the fantasy, storing up the pleasure for the lonely times ahead.

Yesterday he'd taken her riding and had shown her the ranch through his eyes. With Cookie spoiling Evan, they'd even gone fishing in the afternoon, something Kati had rarely done in her life of group homes and foster care. She'd reeled in a nice bass, but Colt's proud smile and teasing wink had made her happiest.

With a deep sigh she carried the day-care plans to her room, sat cross-legged on the bed and tried to concentrate on the real reason she'd come to the Garret Ranch.

When the door burst open, she jumped like a frog in a frying pan. Colt stood in the opening, the look in his eyes one she'd come to recognize. He started toward her.

"You're interfering with my work again." A teasing half grin lifted the corner of his lips.

"Colt, you're all sweaty."

"And hot." He tossed his hat on the floor. "I'm real hot."

He wasn't kidding. The heat emanating from him would have fried an egg.

"Let me get you something cold to drink."

She started up from the bed.

"Later."

With a wicked chuckle, he tumbled her backward, following her down with a shower of kisses. He tasted of salt and sun and desire, a delicious combination that set Kati's senses reeling.

"You have to stop doing this," she murmured around his seeking mouth, not wanting him to ever stop.

"Why?" He lifted up on his elbows and grinned mischievously. "You're not starting to find me attractive, are you?"

"No, of course not." She wasn't starting to find him attractive. He'd always been way beyond attractive.

"Shoot." He fell to the side, taking her hand with him. "So if I can't kiss you, then tell me where you went today."

All afternoon he'd kept one eye on the driveway while he'd repaired fences. Even the usually distracting task of instructing interns in the fine art of fence stretching hadn't taken his mind off Kati. The longer she was gone, the more vexed he became. As soon as her Toyota chugged through the gate, he'd tossed his tools into the truck and called it a day. The other men had teased him knowingly, and the college girls giggled, but by then he didn't care if it was broadcast on the evening news. He wanted to know where she'd gone. That was all. She was his wife and he had a right to know where she was.

"Did Evan have another doctor's appointment that I'd forgotten about?" He reached for the long tumble of hair flowing over her shoulders, loving the silky feel between his fingers.

"I went to the bank."

"The bank?" His hand stilled.

"The loan papers are on your desk, along with the land contract and blueprints of Kati's Angels. I'll need your signature for the collateral, but as soon as the place is up and running, it will stand for the loan, and our arrangement will be complete."

She looked enormously pleased with herself, a fact that disturbed him no end.

"You sure didn't let any grass grow under your feet."

"I wanted you to know I'm keeping my end of the bargain." With a puzzled expression Kati raised herself up, leaning over him so that her hair fell forward onto his chest. "That's what you wanted, what we agreed upon, isn't it?"

"Well, yeah. Sure it is." But it sort of stuck in his craw that she found him so repulsive she'd hightailed into town this soon after the wedding.

"Mr. Pope, the banker, said the loan approval should come very quickly, considering your strong collateral and the need for a good day-care center in Rattlesnake. Then we'll start the building process, and in no time at all, Kati's Angels will be up and running and you'll be a free man again."

He searched her face, caught the excitement in her words. She couldn't wait to escape him, was that it? Well, fine and dandy. Freedom was exactly what he wanted. The sooner she got that loan and built that day-care thing, the sooner she would be out of his life. A deal was a deal. She got her business; he got his life back. He was a bachelor, after all, a bachelor born and bred. He planned to die that way, too. And if he didn't get off this bed and away from Kati right now, he would die a lot quicker than he'd ever planned on.

Chapter Eight

"Colt!" Kati's shriek ripped through him like a bullet. The razor in his hand jerked upward, nicking a chunk from his chin. A drop of blood oozed out, but he ignored it. After three months of living with Kati, he knew she didn't scream without reason. Something terrible had happened. He threw the razor at the mirror and tore out of the bathroom.

"What's wrong, Kati?" he bellowed, head throbbing from the adrenaline rush.

"It's Evan. Hurry."

Good grief almighty, the baby! Something was wrong with his boy.

Colt galloped down the hall toward the sound of Kati's voice. Where was she? The den maybe? Far in the back of the house?

The pounding in his chest expanded until he thought he would explode. He raced around the end of the hall and burst into the den, ready to fight tooth and toenail to protect what was his.

Kati stood in the middle of the room, hopping up and down, excitement emanating from every pore.

"Look, he's crawling. Evan is crawling."

Colt nearly fainted with relief. His family was safe. Nobody was bloody or unconscious. He collapsed in a chair, trying to calm the sledgehammer bashing at his rib cage. Suddenly the whole episode struck him funny. He'd thought one of them was dying, and here they were happily playing in the den.

"Quick, get the camera." Kati whirled toward him. One hand flew to her lips as she smothered a grin. "I take it you were shaving?"

Colt laughed, reached out and clasped her wrist, pulling her onto his lap.

"Oh, Kati, Kati." She was so cute when she got all worked up about something. He couldn't help himself. He kissed her.

When he left remnants of his shaving cream on her face, he laughed again. Teasingly, he went back for more, smearing the white suds over her face and neck. She felt so right in his arms that he never stopped to consider how normal, how comfortable they'd become as a couple.

"You're something, you know that?" He nuzzled her neck, and the relentless desire leaped to life.

Kati felt it, too, he knew, for she shivered, then sighed softly and pulled away, forcing her attention to the little boy. "The baby, Colt. Look at him."

Keeping an arm around her waist, Colt let her sit up, relishing her happiness, pleased that her lost-kitten look disappeared every time she smiled. Together they watched Evan's chubby legs and arms propel him across the thick carpet. Colt's throat swelled with pride. The little guy had come a long way since that first day.

He was happy, healthy and pretty darn smart. Part of the credit was his, he knew, but most of it was due to Kati's constant loving attention.

She was a natural with babies, instinctively knowing what to do and when to do it. That's why her child-care idea made good business sense. And he felt a lot better knowing she had an adequate means of support after their marriage was over. Not that he was responsible for her. Not at all. But he wasn't a heartless devil, either.

Kati raised her glowing face to his, and their gazes collided. The truth struck Colt right in the belly. He wasn't just trying not to be a heartless devil; he cared about her. Cared a lot, although the word *love* wasn't in his vocabulary so he couldn't possibly love her. But he'd come rushing in here like a wild man the moment she'd cried out, and thinking back to that split second when she'd called his name, he'd thought of Kati and Evan as his. Stupid, stupid, stupid. By forcing his way into Kati's bed, he'd put himself into this situation and upped the chances of an emotional entanglement.

Dumbstruck and confused, he sat there staring into the eyes of his make-believe wife while every fiber of intellect told him to get away and get away fast. Grappling for a lifeline, he blurted out, "How's the center coming?"

Kati's face lit up, and Colt mentally gave himself another kick in the pants. He no more cared about that center than a bull cared about a hen. But Kati's Angels was much safer ground than the aberrant thoughts tormenting him.

"Kati Winslow, you are a fool." The bathroom mirror bounced the words back to her. "Look what your wild scheme has caused."

She'd waltzed into Colt's life thinking she could keep her emotions aloof and her heart safe long enough to build Kati's Angels. Somewhere along the line, her plan had backfired.

She brushed her hair, smoothing it back into a simple ponytail in an effort to keep it out of Evan's grasping fingers. There was no point in putting it up, no matter how hot the weather or how grabby the child. Colt always took it down again.

Colt, Colt. Every waking thought was of Colt. He was fully, deeply entrenched in Kati's heart and mind. The foolish nanny had gone and done the unthinkable. She was so in love with her temporary husband that she could think of little else. Why, oh, why had she agreed to the dangerous idea of sleeping in the same bed with him? Night after night of lying next to him, being touched and kissed and held only to have to turn away before reason was lost in love.

She replaced the hairbrush in the drawer and tidied up the counter. Colt's razor and toothbrush lay to one side. His lime-scented soap now occupied the dish beside her facial cleanser. Over the months of their unconventional marriage, he'd gradually moved more and more items into her quarters. He hadn't asked her to move to his, though the master bed and bath were much larger, and Kati took that as a sign of their temporary arrangement. Colt would live with her in her room, and after she was gone, there would be no trace of her in his. He could close this door and forget he'd ever known her. One more reason to keep their marriage in name only. Losing her heart was bad enough, but if she gave him her body, she wasn't sure she could walk away when Kati's Angels was completed.

The completion of her dream business and all those

little ones waiting for her loving care was the only thing that kept her sane. Soon she would possess something that was permanently and completely her own that no Social Services could whisk away. Though Colt had said nothing, she strongly suspected he'd pulled some strings, because the loan process had sailed through with unexpected speed. Not that she was surprised. He'd been very clear that he wanted her gone, and Kati's Angels would set them both free. She would, at least, be an independent businesswoman who needed nothing and no one but her career.

Today Colt had agreed to go with her to check on the construction's progress. He'd never done that before, and in spite of her self-recriminations, anticipation buzzed in Kati's veins. Spending time alone with Colt was heavenly torture.

Colt gazed at the long brick building surrounded by bare Texas earth and wished to heck he hadn't come. The blasted thing held no appeal for him. He wasn't interested in child-care centers, and he was already a little sick of hearing Kati carry on and on about how wonderful the place would be.

He figured he should be glad to see the center coming along so well, and he was. Of course he was. It was just that Kati seemed so all-fired pleased about the progress that his ego suffered a bit. She couldn't wait to get away from him.

"Hard hats, Kati." A man in white coveralls came toward them carrying the safety equipment. Colt grimaced but tossed his Stetson back inside the truck, exchanging it for the hard hat.

"Colt, this is the construction foreman, Will Benton. He's the man making my dreams come true."

The foreman grinned. "She's always sweet-talking me like that, Mr. Garret. Got every one of these old construction workers at her beck and call."

For some reason Colt didn't see a bit of humor in that. He shook the man's hand, mumbled something about being in a hurry, and guided Kati toward the center's interior.

Inside, a half-dozen carpenters pounded away at rows of what looked like tiny closets.

"Look over here, Kati," another man in white coveralls called to her. "See what you think of this."

Kati hurried toward him, excitement all over her face. She smiled and joked with the man, complimenting him profusely about his work.

"What was so spectacular about a cabinet door?" Colt asked grumpily when Kati came back to where he stood.

"Everybody needs encouragement."

"Yeah. I suppose." Did she have to behave as if the guy was right up there on her Christmas list?

"They *are* doing a fabulous job." She pulled at his arm, unmindful that his original reluctance had grown to belligerence. "Look over here at the sand table."

He went sullenly, listening as Kati flitted from place to place, describing how the center would look when completed.

"This area is the kitchen."

"Uh-huh." The bare walls didn't look like much of anything to him at this point. Pipes and wires poked from the Sheetrock walls without a stove or sink in sight.

"And this is the dining room where the kids will get a real home-cooked meal at little bitty, cute tables, just their size. I'll have colorful curtains on the windows and cartoon-print cloths on the tables."

"Great," he said without enthusiasm. The hard hat, among other things, was starting to annoy him. The blasted thing shifted from side to side and banged against his ears.

"And in this part, I want to set up learning centers. Things like building blocks, puppets, an art table."

He heaved an impatient sigh. "Are we about done here?"

Hurt registered on her face, setting off a reaction in him that wasn't pleasant to witness.

"Look, Kati, I don't give a flying cow chip about learning centers or coat cubbies."

"But I thought you'd be glad to know how well things are coming along."

"I am, but I have a ranch to run. If you want to stay here all day and chitchat with Will and David and whoever the heck all these guys are, then do it. Just make sure you mention that you're a married woman."

Bewilderment clouded her face. "What is that supposed to mean?"

He poked a finger at her. "Ours may not be the real McCoy, but as long as you're Mrs. Colt Garret, I'd appreciate you acting like it. I don't want people laughing behind my back because my wife is running around with some hard hat. Once we're divorced you can do what you want, but until then, you promised to behave like a married woman."

Kati's eyes grew round and moist. She wasn't going to cry, was she?

"Forgive me for forcing you to come here." Blinking rapidly, she averted her gaze, squared her shoulders and murmured, "Let's go home."

She sailed out of the building, stepping over piles of boards with her head held high. Colt knew he'd insulted her, hurt her even, but something about this place set his teeth on edge. He should never have come here.

If she was the crying kind, Kati would have bawled all the way home. Gazing hot-eyed at the passing prairie, she sat against the passenger-side door, her body turned away from Colt. Still uncertain as to what precipitated his bad mood, she didn't know whether to apologize or fight.

In the end she did neither. Colt dropped her at the front door, then squalled the pickup toward open pasture.

"What bee got in his bonnet?" Cookie asked, coming down the hall with Evan in his arms. The smiling baby reached for her, sending a spear of happiness into Kati's heart.

"I'm not really sure." She gathered Evan close, inhaling his sweet baby scent.

"Well, don't worry. All couples have spats. You two will work things out."

"No, Cookie," she admitted. "Things won't ever work out between Colt and me."

"Why, sure they will. You love the ornery cuss, don't you?"

There was no point in denying the truth to Cookie. He'd believed she and Colt were a perfect match all along.

"Am I that obvious?"

"You light up like a firefly every time that boy wanders in the door."

So that was the problem. She'd tried so hard to keep her feelings a secret, but if she was transparent to

Cookie, Colt must also know. And he'd warned her from the start that he didn't believe in love.

Forcing him to go to the child-care center made him feel trapped, tied down, like an old married man. He was straining at the bonds of their agreement. Regardless of how friendly and comfortable they'd become, his behavior today was a warning that she expected too much from their make-believe marriage.

Colt felt like the biggest heel in Texas for hurting Kati's feelings. During the drive home that afternoon, she hadn't said a word and neither had he. Then the minute she'd climbed out of the truck, he'd wanted to call her back and apologize, a senseless move that would only make matters worse. So he'd stormed off like a teenager and let the bad feelings fester.

As a result their relationship had undergone a subtle change in the days since, and he didn't quite know what to do about it. If he had a lick of sense, he'd leave the situation alone and be glad for the thick wall of reserve she'd thrown up between them.

He didn't know what she was so all-fired upset about in the first place. He'd gone to that blasted center with her. And hadn't he offered to send some of the ranch hands to help clean up around the place to speed up her move? But instead of appreciating his peace offering, she'd looked at him as if he'd slapped her.

Now, when he crawled into bed at night, she scooted away, turning a rigid back to him. If he tried to touch her, she scooted another inch. Her reaction should have angered him. Instead, he just wanted her all the more.

With a beleaguered sigh, he stepped out of the shower, dressed, slapped on a bit of aftershave and slipped down the hall to visit Evan. This little ray of sunshine always lifted his spirits.

The baby lay in his crib, hind end in the air, sleeping like—well, sleeping like a baby.

Toys and books covered the floor, an indication that Kati had been reading to him again. Lucky kid. Personally, he would enjoy books a lot more if she'd snuggle up and read to him every night. 'Course he'd like to choose the books—something sexy and romantic—but, considering Kati's state of mind, if he thought along those lines too much, he'd likely implode. Pushing a brightly colored copy of *Noah's Ark* off the rocker, he started to sit. Evan awoke, whimpering.

"Hey, squirt." Colt smiled down into the child's face.

When Evan responded with a smile of his own, Colt's belly did a flip-flop. It did another when the boy reached his chubby little hands upward.

Colt scooped Evan into his arms and set him on the floor. Colt joined him, lured by the child's adoring look and constant babble. Already the little tike was into everything, crawling halfway across the room if he wanted to. As the baby started an impromptu game of pattycake, Colt grinned and joined in.

"You're getting in way too deep, big brother." Jett entered the room, hat in hand, and slid down beside them. "Any word on the mama?"

Colt's gut clenched. "Jace called today. The P.I. found somebody down in Austin who thought they'd heard of her. He's following the lead."

"What will you do if they never find her?"

Colt wound a musical bear and handed it to the smiling baby. He massaged the knot that rose on the back of his neck every time he thought about Evan and Natosha Parker. He'd asked himself that question a thousand times in the last few months, and was as stumped now as ever. Evan was a perfect boy and Colt hated thinking of the time when Natosha Parker would come to reclaim him. Whether he liked to admit it or not, giving him up now, after all this time, would hurt.

"She has to be somewhere, Jett, so we'll find her. The sooner the better."

"But what if you don't? You gonna keep him indefinitely?"

"Kati wants to go on caring for him after her center is finished." The knot got bigger, and he rolled his shoulders to loosen it. "She loves him, and he adores her. We can work something out."

Jett laughed softly, humorlessly. "That's another fine mess you've gotten into."

"Kati?" Colt shook his head. "Nah. Kati wants out of this predicament as badly as I do."

"You think?"

Colt avoided Jett's piercing gaze. "Trust me, little brother. Kati wants no part of me. She spends more time at that blasted center of hers or with Juana Rodriquez than she does here."

"She's hanging out with the foreman's wife?"

"Yeah. Did you know Kati speaks Spanish?" He'd been furious to discover this from Cookie. Why hadn't she told him herself? "And now she's over there half the time, helping Juana with her English, talking about babies, doing all that female stuff women do when they have babies around."

He got mad just thinking about all the ways she avoided him. Maybe she'd been telling the truth about not finding him attractive.

"So there's nothing between the two of you?" Jett asked.

"Nothing worth talking about." Lately, discussing Evan and Kati stuck in his craw like a chicken bone. He swiped a piece of fuzz from Evan's mouth and steered the subject to safer ground. "How's the shoulder?"

Gingerly, Jett rotated it. "Nearly ready to grab hold of another wild bull."

"How soon?"

Jett laughed. "Why? You trying to get rid of me?"

"Nah, just thought if you make that rodeo in Mesquite next week, we could come up and watch."

"We?" He quirked an eyebrow.

"Me, Cookie, Kati, Evan. All of us."

"Cookie hates rodeos."

"Kati likes them." Why the heck had he mentioned that?

Jett gave him a funny look. "Does she, now?"

Evan whacked at Colt with the silent stuffed animal. Absently he rewound the bear and handed it back to the child. "Did you know she's a pretty good horsewoman? She doesn't think so, but she is."

An ornery grin lifted Jett's mouth. "Is that a fact?"

"She learned in one of those group homes. Seems they had a program for foster kids where some rancher took them riding during the summer and on weekends."

"Kind of sad, ain't it, for a nice girl like Kati to grow up that way, without any family, I mean." Jett slapped his brother's knee. "You ain't much, but I'm glad I have you."

"Yeah, I agree. I think that's why Kati's so protective about Evan." He swiveled around and pulled the crawling Evan away from the open doorway. "Do you know what she suggested? She wants me to start a program out here like that for foster kids.''

"You mean, teach kids to ride?"

"She says those were some of the best times she can remember.''

"You gonna do it?"

"Ah, I don't know. Things are kind of busy right now.''

"Kati would be good at something like that. Shoot, it would be a great way to use those college kids in the summer, and Billy Joe and some of the other boys could help out. You ought to give the idea some thought.''

Kati would be long gone before he had time for such a program. If the project happened at all, it would be without Kati's help.

Jett pushed up from the floor and strolled to the door, sliding his hat into place. "Speaking of Billy Joe, I better get moving. The two of us are gonna check out the new band over at the honky-tonk and give all the women a thrill. You want to go with us?'' He slapped his hand against the door frame. "'Scuse me, bro, I forgot. You're a married man, now. No more good times.''

He laughed and walked out.

"Hey.'' Colt jumped up from the floor and barreled after him. "Wait a minute, Jett.''

Jett paused, his cocky grin daring Colt to come along.

He wasn't really a married man. Heck, Kati wouldn't even kiss him anymore, much less let him make their marriage real. Why shouldn't he go out with the boys? He'd been stuck here on the ranch for months, first with a baby, then with a wife, neither of which he'd asked for. Kati didn't want him around, anyway. He was cleaned up and ready to go, so why not get back to living his own life right now?

"What time are you leaving?"

"He went where?"

"Him and Jett and Billie Joe went to that beer joint over in Rattlesnake. Anyways, that's what they said."

Kati sat at the supper table staring at the chairs left empty by Colt and his brother. Never once in the months since she'd arrived had Colt gone anywhere without telling her. That he'd gone to a country-Western bar shocked her no end.

All through the meal, Cookie shot her anxious glances as though expecting her to break into a million little pieces for him to sweep off the terra-cotta tile. For that reason alone, she stiffened her spine and chattered away about the day care, Evan and anything else that popped into her head. Anything to keep from thinking about Colt dancing the night away in some other woman's arms.

Though the food tasted like cardboard, she forced it down, then pretended all was well while helping Cookie clear away the dishes. Once the last plate was dried and carefully stacked away, she fed Evan, then turned on the television. Nothing there held her attention as thoughts strayed to Colt, in a bar, holding another woman. A heavy sickness lay in the pit of her stomach.

She'd always been alone, but tonight she was lonely. Lonely for the one man who fulfilled her in a thousand ways. No matter how busy she'd tried to be in the past week, every waking thought had been of Colt and of how much she missed his kisses and his arms around her. Only self-preservation and the knowledge of how badly he wanted her gone had kept her from turning to him in the night.

Clicking off the TV, she gathered Evan into her arms and kissed him. Even this precious baby would be gone before long, and another piece of her heart would shatter and crumble.

"I wasn't supposed to love you, Evan," she whispered, gripping him in tender-fierce desperation. "Any more than I was supposed to love Colt."

She reluctantly put the sleeping child in the crib, thankful for the peaceful way he rested, secure for now in her love—and Colt's.

She stepped to the hallway and listened, but the house was quiet without the teasing voices of the Garret brothers. Around midnight, when Colt still hadn't returned, she turned off the lamp and went to sleep in the too-big, too-empty bed, regretting all the times she'd turned away from him.

Colt tiptoed into the room sometime around two in the morning, blurry-eyed and exhausted, grateful to be home at last. Undressing without the light, he slipped into bed and wrapped himself around Kati. She made a soft mewling sound and stirred. Taking that as a good sign, he nuzzled her neck. Man, oh, man, she smelled delicious, like flowers blowing on a summer breeze.

He pulled her closer, pressing into her exquisitely soft flesh, and let his hands roam beneath her T-shirt, caressing her awake. She rolled toward him, murmuring something, and he closed his mouth over hers.

Mmmmm. She tasted as sweet as honey.

Suddenly, with no warning, she gave a great shove and sent him tumbling out of the bed.

"Hey!" he blinked in surprise. The room spun crazily as the lamp clicked on, blinding him for a second. Kati leaned over him, her hair hanging in glorious disarray. She looked madder than any woman he'd ever known. And much sexier.

"Get out of my bed," she said through gritted teeth.

"I am." His head wouldn't be still, but he was fairly certain he was on the floor, not in bed with his warm, soft woman.

"You know what I mean. Get out, Colt."

"What are you so mad about?"

She yanked the fallen sheets from his grip. "I'm not mad. It's just time you started sleeping in your own bed."

"But I want to sleep with you," he said piteously.

"You smell like beer."

"Is that what you're mad about?" He scooted away from her frightening stance, levered himself against the wall and stood up. The room circled above him. "I'm not drunk if that's what you mean."

"Get out." She picked up a fuzzy house shoe and whacked him on the arm. "Now."

"Hey!" He edged toward the door, keeping one eye on the shoe that he fully expected to come sailing in his direction any minute now.

Sure enough, she let fly with the slipper. He ducked, then darted out the door and down the hall to his own room.

Confounded woman. Let her sleep alone. See if he cared. His room was bigger, anyway. He didn't need some flowery-smelling woman getting her hair all tangled around him so that he couldn't even roll over, and he wouldn't have to suffer all night from terminal frustration over a woman who wouldn't let him love her.

He flopped onto the king-size bed, closing his eyes.

His head spun crazily. Three beers. Well, maybe five or six. That shouldn't make his head spin like the Tilt-A-Whirl at Six Flags.

He turned onto his side. Hell's bells, this bed was hard as a rock. Had it always been like this? He flipped his pillow over and pounded a fist into it. Caesar leaped onto the bed, sniffed Colt's mouth, then turned around and sat on his face. Blasted smart-aleck cat.

He was in for a long night.

By the time he stumbled to the breakfast table the next morning, he was sorry he'd lived through the night. His head hurt. His mouth tasted like a cow smelled. And his stomach pitched like a bucking bronc. He slithered into the chair, dejected and grouchy.

"Throwed you out, did she?" Cookie sloshed a mug of coffee in front of him.

Colt didn't bother to lift the cup. He bent his head and sipped at the scalding brew.

"Serves you right. A married man's got no business gallivanting off to honky-tonks with a bunch of rowdy cowboys."

Colt leaned his throbbing head on the table and mumbled to the tile floor.

"I've told you, we are not married. Not for real. Not forever. Strictly business."

"Tell it to that sweet little gal." The cook slapped a plate of greasy eggs in front of his boss. The sound reverberated through the wood and nearly ruptured an artery in Colt's pounding brain.

With a grimace of pain, he raised his head.

"The whole thing was her idea." Stomach lurching, he averted his gaze, pushed the disgusting plate away and covered it with a napkin.

"Hmpf. Then how come her eyes was all red and puffy this morning?"

Colt's heart stopped beating for a full second. "She'd been crying?"

Cookie's accusing glare served as the answer.

Colt frowned. He wouldn't have gone if he'd known she'd get upset about it. Heck, fifteen minutes after he got to the noisy, smelly place, he wanted to come home. Why would any man in his right mind choose a smoky barroom over Kati?

That was a good question. Why had he gone there in the first place?

"I've never seen Kati cry before."

"That's 'cause she does it where nobody can see. Tries to pretend like she don't care. All bottled up inside, she is. Scared to death of being hurt."

Colt couldn't fathom Kati crying, but then, he couldn't imagine her throwing him out of bed last night, either, and she'd done it.

"Maybe she's sick." God, he hoped not. He'd take her to the best specialist in Texas.

"Sick of you." With a flick of his wrist, Cookie whipped the napkin from the greasy eggs and shoved them under Colt's nose. He grinned malevolently when his victim bolted from the table.

"Cookie, you're fired."

"No, I ain't."

"How come?" Colt stood at the far end of the table, rubbing the back of his neck, wondering what he could do to work his way back into Kati's good graces.

"Jett's way ahead of you. Said you'd most likely fire everybody on the place today, but for us not to pay you no mind."

So Jett had known he'd had a miserable time last night. "Bunch of smart alecks."

"You gonna feel up to that big doin's this afternoon?"

The sudden change of subjects drew a moan from Colt's aching head. He'd completely forgotten about today's town-wide festival.

One more strike against him. Though Kati's Angels wasn't complete, Kati had thought the annual Lonestar Celebration in Rattlesnake would be a perfect time to get better acquainted with the townspeople and to do some simple advertising. She'd hired a couple of teenagers to walk in the parade, pushing an antique baby carriage loaded with literature and balloons. They'd hand helium balloons to the children and pamphlets about the center to the adults.

The plan required little or no action from Colt. Trouble was, by getting involved with the parade Kati had gotten herself all wound up over the whole celebration.

She'd entered Evan in the beautiful baby contest, which she was certain he would win. Furthermore, Colt was required, according to Kati, to record the entire event on video. Fact of the business, he'd looked forward to squiring Kati around, until she'd thrown him out of bed.

To make matters worse, Cookie had been prevailed upon to enter his "famous" chili in the chili cook-off. Colt knew darn well if he didn't show up to eat chili and vote for Cookie's recipe there would be a steady diet of beans and corn bread for the Garret household next week. His stomach rolled at the mere thought of hot, spicy chili.

The entire day was set aside by the citizens of Rattlesnake for fun and socializing. All that was fine and dandy except for one problem—Colt had long ago promised to take Kati and Evan. And he wasn't exactly Kati's favorite person anymore.

"Would you consider shooting me, Cookie?" Colt asked.

"It's crossed my mind," Cookie answered, arms crossed over his aproned belly. "But shootin' you wouldn't do no good. You're too ornery to die. Besides, it'd break Miss Kati's heart, and I ain't about to give that child no more hurt. You've done plenty enough as it is."

"What's that suppose to mean?"

"Never you mind, boss. But you better learn to appreciate her before it's too late."

"I do appreciate her," Colt argued. "If not for Kati, you and I would still be trying to figure out how to get those little shirts over Evan's head without breaking his neck. And we'd be loco from walking the floor when he had the colic."

"That ain't what I mean and you know it. One of these days some cowboy with a brain between his ears instead of in his britches will ride in here and carry her off."

"Like hell!" Colt jerked his head up so fast his brain ricocheted against his skull.

"Well, la-de-da. Maybe you ain't as thickheaded as I thought."

Cookie waited long enough to enjoy Colt's befuddled expression before retreating to the kitchen to begin a batch of chili.

Chapter Nine

"No doubt about it, Evan. You'll be the handsomest baby there."

Kati stood back to admire her handiwork. For the Lonestar Celebration she'd bought a Texas Rangers baseball suit complete with royal-blue cap and tennis shoes. Later, she'd change him into full cowboy regalia for the baby contest. Other mothers might opt for suits or tuxedoes, but Evan was the ward of a rancher and Kati thought he should look the part.

The baby, seeming to sense Kati's pride in him, waved his chubby arms and chattered at her, his mouth wide with happiness. Two tiny white teeth gleamed from the bottom gums, another milestone the nanny had preserved in his baby book.

"Ohh, I love you." Kati swooped him up for a hug.

When the time came for them to part, she prayed the strength and security of her love would be enough to carry him through whatever rough times lay ahead. She never wanted him to feel rootless or abandoned.

If only they had some word on Natosha Parker.

Even that idea caused an ache in Kati's chest. As long as the mother wasn't found, Kati would get to see Evan every day, even after the divorce. But that kind of thinking was selfish, and she loved Evan far too much to deny him his mother's love.

But what if Natosha never returned? Or worse, what if she was found and simply did not want her wonderful baby boy?

"Oh, Evan, what a terrible mess you and I have gotten into." She hugged the child so close he began to squirm, slapping his hands against her chest and shoulder.

"Are you two about ready in here?"

At the sound of Colt's voice, Kati whirled, the baby in her arms. The handsome cowboy leaned lazily against the doorjamb, his face solemn and unreadable. "We still on for the big shindig over in Rattlesnake?"

He showed no signs of anger, but Kati felt the heat rising in her cheeks. Maybe he wasn't angry, but she was. How dare he stagger into her bed after spending the evening in some barroom, most likely in the company of a willing female? A little anger seeped away with the notion that if she'd been more willing maybe Colt wouldn't have felt the need to go elsewhere. And yet he still wanted to take her to the "shindig."

"If you want to come along, it's fine with me," she answered huffily.

Colt's lips quirked. His eyes should have been bloodshot and he should have looked exhausted, but he was gorgeous instead. Dressed in black jeans, boots and hat, with a white-and-black-striped Western shirt opened at his richly tanned neck, he made Kati's mouth water.

"How could I miss seeing Evan crowned the handsomest baby in the whole town of Rattlesnake?"

Her tension eased. If he chose to ignore last night's fiasco, then so be it. He hadn't promised her fidelity any more than she had promised to share her bed indefinitely, she thought bitterly, angry for caring too much. "In that case, let me finish putting my hair up and we'll be ready."

The usually quiet town of Rattlesnake took on a celebratory atmosphere each year during its Lonestar Celebration. The lights and sounds of a traveling carnival, complete with Ferris wheel and midway barkers, filled one side of the town park. The scent of popcorn and corn dogs wafted from the concession trailers. Townsfolk roamed about in frontier garb while country music blared from a bandstand at the end of Main Street.

"Where to first?"

Finding a parking spot on Main Street was impossible so they'd parked the pickup along a side street near the location of Kati's Angels. Colt removed the stroller from the truck bed and helped Kati arrange the baby and his gear inside. Together they strolled toward the center of activities.

"We have another hour until the baby contest." Kati glanced at her watch. "Shall we just walk around and check things out first?"

Colt shrugged. "Lead on, Mrs. Garret."

He'd been charming and warm during the ride to town, ignoring the fight they'd had last night. Now he walked along beside her, making cute remarks. As they passed a booth of Indian crafts, he stopped and searched the display. Finding what he wanted he lifted a small dream catcher from the table, paid for it and handed the trinket to Kati.

"Sweet dreams."

Puzzled, Kati turned the leather bound circle over in her hands. The crisscrossed center looked like a spiderweb. At the bottom a single blue feather dangled from a strip of rawhide. "What do you mean?"

The hint of a smile played around Colt's mouth. "Didn't you have a nightmare last night?"

Running a finger over the soft blue feather, Kati struggled not to smile at Colt's clever way of bringing up their fight. "That was no nightmare."

"Still mad at me?"

"I wasn't mad." Hurt, lonely and absolutely furious when he'd come in smelling like beer and women.

"Yes, you were. Why else would you throw me out of our bed?"

Technically, it was not "our" bed, but Kati chose not to pursue that line of argument. Instead she tried to put her feelings into perspective without revealing the awful truth that she loved him too much to keep pretending.

"Because we've both kept our end of the marriage bargain. In a few weeks I'll be moving out."

"That's the whole point, Kati. You'll soon be gone. Why not enjoy the time we have left?" He leaned close, his cologne stirring thoughts that set her pulse to racing. His voice dropped to a husky undertone. "We could enjoy our remaining time a lot more if you were willing."

The familiar sense of inadequacy pulled at her. If she'd agreed to make love with him, would he have gone out last night? She wanted to, badly, but would loving him make things better or worse? And if she did, could she walk away without suffering the worst pain of her entire life?

Struggling with self-doubts, Kati bent to hand Evan a toy. She let Colt's suggestion remain unanswered and they sauntered on. If Colt was bored and anxious to be rid of his inconvenient wife, why was he playing the perfect date today? Why was he teasing her, buying her things and keeping that warm, muscled arm slung over her shoulders?

"Colt, old buddy." A blond cowboy ambled toward them with a big grin on his face. "How the heck are you, man?"

"Doing good, Case." The men exchanged back slaps and general cowboy insults.

"Who's your lady?" The blond cowboy's gaze drifted from Kati to Evan, his eyes widening in disbelief. "Don't tell me someone roped one of the Garret boys?"

Kati stood frozen to the spot, knowing how much her make-believe husband hated the idea of being "roped."

"'Fraid so, Case. This is Kati, my wife." If Kati hadn't known better, she'd have sworn the introduction rang with pride.

"Well, I'll be danged." Case stared in frank admiration and amazement. "Kati, you must be some kind of woman."

The accursed heat crept up Kati's neck. She had no idea what to say, considering Colt's opinion of their relationship. Especially after last night. Oddly the expression on Colt's face appeared anything but angry.

The cowboy bent toward Evan, chucking him on the chin.

"This boy is the spitting image of his daddy." He straightened and slapped Colt on the back. "You old son of a gun, you. I never would have believed it, but it looks like marriage agrees with you.''

Colt didn't bother to correct the cowboy's wrong impressions. He continued to banter, telling Case he could use a good woman of his own, all the while behaving like a happily married man in love with his wife and child.

As the friends separated and started on down the street, Case called back over his shoulder. "If he isn't good to you, Kati, give ol' Case a holler. I know how to treat a lady right.''

Colt's hand tightened on Kati's shoulder. When she looked up at him for an explanation of his strange behavior, he kissed her on the nose, winked and led the way toward the grandstands where a troupe of cowboys blasted each other in a mock gunfight.

The conversation with Case was only the first of numerous, similar encounters they would have all evening. Everyone who knew either Colt or Kati responded with the same amazed delight, assuming that Evan was their child. Kati left the explaining to Colt, and he continued to surprise her by pretending they were one big happy family. By the time they reached the civic center, for the baby contest, Kati almost felt as if they were.

The baby pageant added to the fantasy. Along with two dozen other mothers, Kati prepared her baby for the competition, dressing him in the cowboy outfit, needlessly wiping his face and hands with a wet towelette, and brushing his fine, dark hair before setting the tiny cowboy hat in place. Colt stood ready with the video camera.

Baby after baby was carried to the stage and introduced, two crying, some gurgling, and a few asleep in their mothers' arms. When Evan's turn came, Kati carried him forward, smiling proudly. Evan, his brown eyes dancing with excitement at all the attention, cooed and waved his chubby arms.

As the judges passed by, Evan turned on his considerable charm, laughing aloud when one woman chucked him under the chin. Feeling as proud as any real mother, Kati carried him back to his seat, certain that everyone was as enamored of Evan as she was.

Amid the general hubbub of crying babies and talking adults, the finalists were announced. One by one, five mothers were asked to bring their babies back up on the stage for the final round of judging. When Evan's name was called, Kati squealed with excitement. The pleasure doubled when she saw her joy and pride reflected in Colt's face.

He lowered the video camera and came toward her.

"Will you let me take him up there?" His eyes glistened like hot fudge.

Kati couldn't have refused if she'd wanted to. After all, he was Colt's ward, not hers. She was only the nanny. In truth, her heart swelled at the notion that Colt would want to do such a thing. With a smile and nod, she handed him the boy. The baby lunged toward Colt, happily patting the big man's shoulder.

With his cowboy strut, Colt carried Evan to the front and settled into a chair. Kati's throat thickened with emotion. Two dark, handsome males, they looked for all the world like father and son.

The need for family closed around her as she watched the two most important people in her life through the viewfinder of a camera. She wanted to preserve the moment, not only on film, but in her heart. Very soon memories would be all she'd have of this temporary family she loved so much.

She swallowed the lump in her throat, but it lodged painfully in her chest as she watched. With one dark, strong arm circling Evan's waist, Colt's smiling mouth moved above the baby's ear. He must have been singing "Patty-cake" because Evan joyfully clapped his chubby little hands and giggled. It was a sight to behold—the big, handsome cowboy gently playing with a baby.

As a thin woman in a prairie dress stepped to the microphone to announce the winners, Kati held her breath, praying for Evan to win. She didn't know why winning was so important, but it was. If his mother was never found, someday he'd need to know that he was a special and wonderful baby. In this small way, he would realize that he'd been loved.

One by one, the runners-up were called, and they moved forward to receive their prizes and have their pictures taken for the newspaper. Then the moment came when the first-place winner's name echoed across the squealing PA system. Kati bit her lip.

"First place prizes for the Most Beautiful Baby contest go to…Evan Parker."

Camera trembling, heart nearly bursting, Kati watched Colt carry his ward to center stage. Flashbulbs popped, startling Evan who blinked rapidly and tried to find the source. When Colt whispered something to the child and pointed in Kati's direction, Evan's mouth flew open again in a wide baby smile. He bounced up and down in Colt's arms, his tiny hands reaching for her. The longing in Kati was almost unbearable.

From behind her a voice said, "Go on up there with them. They'll want a picture of the whole family."

The words sounded like music to Kati's family-starved soul. "But I'm filming…."

"Go on. I'll tape it for you." The familiar-looking woman took the camera and gave Kati a gentle shove. Later, she wouldn't recall moving toward the stage, but she did remember the moment Colt and Evan saw her coming. Evan bounced and bobbed excitedly in Colt's arms. Colt's white teeth glinted against the tan of his skin. He shifted the baby to one arm and held out his other, welcoming Kati into a group embrace. It felt like coming home.

Moisture pooled in the corners of her eyes. Had she been the teary kind, she would have cried with joy. Evan *was* special. All the world, at least the good citizens of Rattlesnake, agreed. With a video and pictures to remind him, Evan would never have to doubt the value of his existence.

"Mr. and Mrs. Garret," a photographer said, interrupting their joyous celebration. "If you'll please turn this way with your son, we'd like to take some pictures of him receiving his prizes."

Kati graciously accepted a savings bond from each of the town's three banks, a certificate for a family photo at a local studio and numerous gift certificates from merchants around town. The prizes were nice, but to Kati they were not nearly as important as the honor.

Finally the crowd began to break up, and amid congratulations, Kati and Colt made their way out of the building. Evan, who'd had all the noise and attention he could stand, began to cry fitfully as he was placed in his stroller.

"You think he's hungry?" Colt looked from the baby to Kati.

"Hungry, hot and tired." She handed Evan a bottle, then removed his hat and boots, smoothing the damp brown hair away from his forehead. "He'll feel better now."

"I'm glad he didn't do that during the contest."

"He's a big ham, like his—" She'd almost said, Like his father. "He knows how to work an audience."

"Yeah, he was great, wasn't he?"

"Yes, and those mamas thought you were pretty special, too." She adjusted the purse on her arm and pushed the stroller forward. "That didn't hurt the voting any."

"You think?" His eyes danced.

Kati laughed. "You had to know how sweet you looked—a big strong cowboy playing patty-cake with his baby."

He shrugged. "I wanted him to win."

Kati slowed the stroller to observe Colt's expression. He loved the boy. Any fool could see it. Whether he was willing to admit his feelings or not was another matter entirely. And even if he admitted the truth, was he willing to give up his wild, bachelor ways to permanently care for Evan?

"What are you staring at?" Colt raised a hand to his face. "Do I have baby goo on my chin?"

"You're a nice man, Mr. Garret." She pulled his hand away and touched his cheek. "But, don't worry, your secret is safe with me."

"Does this mean I can come back to your bed tonight? I promise to be good." He pulled her against his side and lowered his voice seductively. "As good as you'll let me be."

"Oh, you." Kati shook her head in mock dismay, warmth creeping across her cheeks. With the wonderful feeling of family all around her, tonight she struggled harder than ever to hold back the tide of love she felt for this man.

Pulling away, she headed toward the concession stands, purposely switching the subject to safer ground. "I'm starving."

"Me, too." His gaze scraped over her, his meaning clear. He pumped his eyebrows and grinned.

Kati whacked him playfully on the arm. "Would you please stop it? We're in a crowd of people."

"All of whom are jealous because I have the most desirable woman in town walking beside me."

When he talked like that she was helpless against the flood of emotion washing through her. Though he was only joking, the words were powerful balm to her bruised self-concept. Desire was a poor substitute for love, but it was preferable to nothing. Last night had forced her to admit she longed for Colt's attention. Avoiding him had only increased the craving.

"If I'm all that, you should feed me so I won't starve to death before we get home."

He held up both palms. "Okay, you win. What's your pleasure? Besides me, of course." He laughed at her mutinous expression and backed away. "Hot dogs? Barbecue on a bun? Indian tacos? There's junk food galore. Take your pick."

"Indian tacos." She pointed to a booth selling the specialty of fried bread smothered in ground beef, brown beans, lettuce, tomato, onion, cheese and a dollop of *picanté* sauce.

"Sounds good." Colt took over the stroller, leading the way to a folding table beside the booth. "You and Evan get settled. I'll get the food."

He motioned toward a thunderhead in the distance as

he moved away. "Looks like we could get a storm later on."

The air was rife with music and laughter and the smells of food. With a light heart, Kati adjusted the shade on Evan's stroller so the now-sleeping baby could rest while she and Colt had supper. With the air so humid, Colt could be right about a thunderstorm.

"Sure a fine little cowboy you've got there," a smiling man said as he and his male companion threw a leg over the wooden bench and sat down across from Kati.

"Thank you," Kati said, proudly. "He won the most beautiful baby contest today."

"With a mama as pretty as you, I'm not a bit surprised." The man was friendly, not at all insulting or insinuating, but Kati, unused to such comments didn't know how to reply. She fiddled with Evan's stroller instead.

"Kati." Colt stood beside the table, a paper plate heaped with food in each hand. Frowning, he looked from the two men to Kati and back again. "These two guys bothering you?"

"No, of course not. They were admiring Evan's cowboy outfit."

"Didn't sound that way to me." He placed the food on the table, but remained standing, his body tense. The expression on his face was as dark and threatening as the distant thunderhead.

Kati's heart hammered. What on earth had gotten into Colt? Why did he care if two harmless fellows said hello?

Both men rose from the table and backed away. "Hey, man, no harm intended. We were just talking to the lady."

"Go talk to somebody else," Colt growled.

Kati grabbed his stiff, unyielding arm. "Colt, sit down. Stop acting like a juvenile."

Not until the two strangers ambled away, muttering to each other, did Colt obey.

"Why did you do that?" Kati demanded as soon as the men were out of hearing range.

"A man protects his property." Colt jabbed a plastic fork into the fry bread and ripped off a piece.

Property was the wrong word to use. All her life, Kati had felt exactly like that—an inanimate object shifted from owner to owner like a used end table.

"I am not your property," she said hotly.

"You're my wife," he said without looking up from the taco.

"Not for long."

"So we're back to that, are we?"

"We've never left that, Colt."

"All right. Time out. I'm sorry, okay?" He tossed his hat onto the bench and turned to face her, pulling her hand into his. "I thought those jerks were bothering you, and I overreacted. We were having a great time before they showed up. Can we call a truce and go back to that?"

Kati sat stiffly, reluctant to give in but longing for a return to the camaraderie they'd shared all afternoon. Colt's behavior confused and distressed her. She didn't understand why he was so possessive over a make-believe wife.

"Please," he pleaded, expression sincere. "I'm trying to make up for being such a bum last night. I'll even buy you a candied apple."

A reluctant smile pulled at Kati's lips. Try as she might, she couldn't stay angry with Colt Garret. Love was like that.

"I'd rather have a chocolate frozen yogurt."

."You got it." He tapped her on the end of the nose. "A double dip."

"And you have to eat one, too." She knew he hated the stuff.

"Yuck!" He clasped his forehead in mock agony. "You drive a hard bargain, woman, but, okay. Anything to further the cause of world peace."

The ugly moment passed and both turned to their tacos, relieved to be teasing and light once more.

"The street dance cranks up at sundown." Colt dumped another spoon of *picanté* sauce on his plate and stirred it around. "Do you want to go?"

"I'm not much of a dancer, but I'd enjoy the music."

"Honey, you're with one of the Garret brothers. Every woman's a good dancer in my arms."

Kati lifted his Stetson from the bench and gazed inside. "How do you get that big head of yours inside this little hat?"

Colt threw his head back and laughed. "Ah, Kati, you're a delight."

Taking his hat, he placed it on his head and swung his legs over the table. Nudging his chin toward the west, he said, "Sun's going down, cooling things off. If we're lucky, we can make the dance and won't get rained on until later."

After disposing of their plates and cups, they headed toward the bandstand set up on main street. Already, rocking country music vibrated the airwaves, drawing a crowd.

Colt and Kati stood on the sidelines watching and listening as couples made their way into the street where they scooted boots and two-stepped around the pavement. The dancing was fun and lively, but when Colt offered to teach her, Kati shook her head.

"The baby." She raised her voice above the music. "There's no one to watch him."

In actuality Evan was an excuse. The undulating couples on the street knew what they were doing, while Kati felt awkward and out of place, terrified of making a fool of herself. Colt, with his natural grace and devil-may-care personality, would be a fantastic dancer, but Kati had never had an opportunity to learn. She didn't want to embarrass him with an inept partner.

"Dance with someone else, Colt," she shouted close to his ear. "I don't mind, really."

He shook his head, but at the very next break, a pretty blond cowgirl in tight jeans and a Pro Rodeo T-shirt approached and asked him to dance.

"Go on," Kati urged. "It's okay."

In her heart she hoped he'd refuse, but he didn't. After a moment of indecision, he shrugged and stepped out on the floor with the blonde.

Just as she suspected, he was a good dancer, expertly guiding his partner around in a lively two-step. When the music shifted into a slow dance, he touched the brim of his hat and started to walk away. The blonde grabbed his arm, pulling him back. He glanced toward Kati. Though she wanted him to refuse, Kati wouldn't make his decision for him. Pretending to check on the still-sleeping Evan, she avoided Colt's questioning gaze.

When she turned back, Colt had the cowgirl in his arms, moving her in slow circles around the floor. Halfway through the song, the woman rested her head on Colt's shoulder and moved closer to his body.

Paralyzed by the pain sluicing through her, Kati couldn't tear her gaze away. Colt was a fun-loving, high-living cowboy who'd been locked away with an unwanted wife and child for months. Why hadn't she realized how much he would miss the attention of other women? He belonged out there with the crowd and the ladies.

Swallowing hard against the tears clogging her throat, Kati ached to be the woman in his arms. But when the song ended and Colt came toward her, she was determined not to show her suffering.

"That looked like fun," she said brightly.

"Are you sure you didn't mind?"

"Of course not," she lied, forcing a smile. She would not, could not, succumb to the jealousy tearing at her insides like a wild animal's teeth. "Great dancers like you Garret brothers shouldn't be standing around on the sidelines. It wouldn't be fair to the women of the world."

Colt studied her long and hard, his face unsmiling. "I suppose."

Thunder rumbled overhead. In the distance, lightning leaped from cloud to cloud. The crowd of dancers and spectators gazed upward, gauging the opportunity for a much-needed rain.

"Probably just dry lightning," one man near them suggested. "We couldn't get lucky enough to get a good rain this time of year."

The rest of the crowd concurred, murmuring over the "blasted Texas dry spell."

In the midst of all this talk, the skies suddenly opened, dumping gallons of cold water onto the hot crowd. Scattering like frightened quail, the people ran for cars and trucks and overhangs, shouting and squealing, half in delight, half in dismay.

Evan awoke with a start, screaming in fright at the noise and the rain drenching his stroller.

"Grab him," Colt yelled. "I'll get the rest."

Kati obeyed, running with Evan toward the truck. Though she tried to protect the baby with her body, by the time she'd covered the four blocks, both she and Evan were drenched. Not far behind, Colt followed with the stroller, diaper bag, camera and all Evan's prizes. He, too, was soaked to the skin.

Inside the pickup truck, a combination of wet clothes and hot bodies fogged the windows, making the interior muggy and uncomfortable. Colt started the engine.

"I don't know whether we need heat or air," he admitted, clicking on the overhead light.

"Let me get Evan out of these clothes before you turn on anything."

She dug into the diaper bag, glad that its plastic exterior had kept the extra clothing dry. Evan, lying on the seat, kicked and fussed as she stripped him of the sopping cowboy garments and replaced them with a soft cotton one-piece pajama.

"Do you want to wait out the cloudburst?"

"Not particularly, but it's up to you." Jealousy, totally out of proportion considering their situation, gnawed at her. She kept seeing him moving in slow circles, the blonde pressed against him. "You were the one having so much fun at the dance."

He didn't deny it.

"Most likely the dance is over. No band is going to keep their equipment out in the rain."

"Truthfully, I'll be glad to head home. These sticky, wet clothes are driving me nuts, anyway."

"I think they're bothering me a whole lot more than they are you."

Kati raised startled eyes at the husky note in Colt's voice. Following the direction of his suddenly heated gaze, she noted the condition of her sundress. A pale yellow cotton, the once-modest garment had become transparent. Little was hidden from Colt's intense stare.

"Hell's bells, Kati," Colt breathed, reaching for her. "Come here."

"Go back to your dance partner." The words flew out before she could stop them.

He paused. "You jealous?"

"Of course not."

"Liar." He grasped her shoulders and tugged. "I was jealous when those two guys flirted with you at the taco stand."

"You were?"

"Killer jealous." He looked puzzled at the admission. "I don't want any other cowboy touching you."

Kati's foolish heart relished Colt's reluctant admission. Was he saying, in his own way, that he cared for her? Scared to even think the word *love,* lest this moment vanish like the fog on the windshield, Kati scooted toward him.

"I was jealous, too," she admitted.

A triumphant groan issued from Colt and in the next minute Kati was in his arms.

He crushed her to him, pulling her across his lap to lean against the steering wheel. Lovingly trapped there, Kati surrendered to the pleasure of his hungry, demanding mouth as his lips scorched over hers.

The damp clothes, the heated air, the dark, confined space added intensity to their ardor. Longing to make him forget the blond dance partner, Kati returned his kisses, letting her fingers explore the warm flesh beneath his cold, wet shirt. The time had come, she knew.

And even if she regretted the decision later, she had to know Colt's love while she could.

Colt's hands pressed at her, urging her down on the seat. Excitement tinged his voice as he chanted her name.

Someone rapped on the window. "Hey, cowboy, take it somewhere else."

Embarrassed, they leaped apart, their heavy breathing the only sound inside the truck. Colt ran a frustrated hand through his hair and rasped out, "Let's go home."

Shifting the truck into gear, he added with a wry grin, "If we can make it that far."

Chapter Ten

All the way home thick, heavy, yearning tension crackled inside the truck's cab. When they entered the house, Colt followed Kati down the hall, kissing her neck, murmuring sweet desire into her ear until she was certain she'd ignite at any moment. Once they'd put Evan down for the night, Colt swept her into his arms and carried her to the bedroom.

Slowly, he slid her down his body until she was standing in front of him. Eyes holding hers, he cupped both her shoulders, letting his hands slide sensually down to her fingertips. Kati trembled from the sheer tenderness of his seduction.

"Colt, please," she breathed, longing to say so much more. The hammering in her chest took on a new dimension. Please touch me. Please love me. Please don't break my heart.

Only his fingers caressed her, making slow circles on her arms. He wasn't holding her, wasn't forcing her. She could step away and out that door if she so desired.

But Colt's liquid brown eyes begged her to stay. And this time she knew she would. Oh, how she wanted to show him her love, to wipe away the memory of any other woman he'd ever known.

"Kati, Kati." His voice was husky, mesmerizing, longing. "You're so beautiful."

A purl of response welled up inside her. He'd called her beautiful again.

"You are, too," she said shyly, lifting her gaze from his hard, muscled chest.

He chuckled softly. "Men aren't beautiful."

"You are." Of their own accord, her fingers fulfilled the fantasy she'd had only seconds before, trailing to caress the smooth, satin steel of Colt's chest. At her touch, a quiver ran through him. With a rush of feminine pride that she could make him tremble, Kati splayed her hands across his chest.

A totally male sound, half groan, half growl, escaped Colt. Kati was making it very hard for him to take his time.

Easy, boy, he reminded himself. Take it very slow and easy. You've waited this long. Do everything right. Kati's worth the effort.

He raised his hands to cup her jaw, pulling her by degrees closer to him. She came willingly, increasing his certainty that she wanted this as much as he did. For all her claims of finding him unattractive, he knew better, but he wanted her to admit it. Just as he wanted so much to please her, to take care of her, to remove the haunted look from her gray eyes.

"You have amazing hair." His lips gently grazed the wisps that had fallen loose around her face. "So gorgeous."

One by one he pulled the pins out of her carefully

upswept French braid. When the glorious hair tumbled down, he combed his fingers through it, setting her scalp atingle. Then he pulled the long, flowing tresses over her shoulders, skimming his fingertips across her breasts in the process.

A tiny gasp escaped Kati's lips. Odd how so little could feel like so much. How the barest touch of this man's hand stirred a need deep in her soul.

This man. Only this man had that power. This man who'd admitted jealousy, who'd given her independence, who'd shown his caring in a hundred ways. He cared for her more than she'd ever dreamed possible and tonight it was enough. She loved him, needed him and, regardless of the future, she wanted to have this precious memory with him—only him.

Colt was her husband, after all. Would she ever have another opportunity to be loved this way? Even for a while?

He pulled her to him then, flush with the long thighs and firm belly. His hand skimmed her back. His lips trailed a path along her jaw, down her neck. He murmured soft unintelligible sounds of longing.

Awash in sensation, Kati clung to the hard contours of his body, her head back, eyes closed, welcoming the tender assault of his mouth.

He was beautiful, this husband of hers. Beautiful and tender.

Her *husband*. The word rattled around inside her mind. She was married to this man with the hot, seeking mouth and hands. Married. All the months of fighting against love and passion had culminated in this one moment. Colt was right. They should enjoy the best part of marriage while they could.

"Colt." Her legs trembled so much that she was sure they'd give way. "I haven't done…"

"Shh. I know." Warm, callused fingers worked magic over her skin. "It's okay, sweetheart. I won't hurt you. I'd never hurt you. Trust me."

The zipper of her dress sounded. Then the damp, thin garment fell away and fluttered to the floor.

Colt scooped her into his arms and gently followed her down on the bed. He lay suspended above her until her eyes opened. A soft smile grazed his lips as he watched the parade of emotions across her lovely face. Uncertainty. Passion.

"You're so very special, Mrs. Garret." He was surprised to think that. He was even more surprised that he actually thought of her as Mrs. Garret. She was his wife, the only one he would ever have, and he wanted this moment to matter for her, to be special and wonderful. The thought that had once appalled him now stirred him deeply. Kati was his and his alone.

He nudged her mouth with his. Her lips fell open, welcoming. Forcing his needy body to go slowly, he accepted the invitation to kiss her. She was so sweet. As sweet as the hint of ice cream lingering on her tongue. And the scent of her. Warm, sexy, as fresh and clean as Evan's baby powder.

Gently, carefully, he stroked her petal-soft skin, drawing sighs and moans from her that nearly drove him wild. Every part of her was so soft. And he wanted her so badly it scared him.

Blood pounded in Kati's ears. Her body pulsed. Colt Garret, her husband, the man she loved was holding her, loving her. She was a butterfly eager to leave the cocoon and fly free.

When she thought she could bear the sweet agony no

longer, Colt's warm, sensuous mouth pulled away to whisper, "I don't want to hurt you, Kati. Are you sure?"

Her answer came in an innocent arching of her body and reaching of her arms. Colt took that as a yes.

Kati couldn't move. Slowly opening her eyes, she discovered why. Colt, his tanned body encased in the tangle of sheets, had flung an arm across her chest and a leg over her thighs. Unwilling to wake him, she lay still. He was wonderful to look at, this man who'd stolen her heart, and she needed time to think.

A dozen emotions ebbed and flowed as she came to grips with what had happened. Colt had been as gentle and giving as a lover could be, though for all the love they'd shared last night, he'd never said the words she so desperately wanted to hear. What had become of her resolve to keep this a marriage in name only? And what would happen between them now?

She'd come here to gain her independence, to secure a future in business. The last thing she'd intended to do was fall in love. Now she'd put herself in the position of being Colt's...what? His wife? His lover? Nothing could be the same now no matter how much they wanted to keep this marriage a temporary arrangement.

A pair of chocolate eyes drifted open beside her. Colt, naked and emerging from sleep, was a sight to behold. He levered up on one elbow and gazed down at her.

Just one look sent Kati's heart into an arrhythmia. The heated blush started at her toes and seeped all the way to the top of her head. Colt followed it, smiling gently.

He pressed a kiss to her forehead. "Sleep well?"

Sleep? Had they slept at all?

"Mmm," she answered noncommittally. "Did you?"

He laughed, the pure rich baritone setting her pulses aflutter. "No, I didn't, but I'm not complaining." Tilting her chin with one hand, brows knit together in concern, he asked, "You okay?"

"More than okay," she said honestly.

Expression sweetly earnest, he cupped her face, stroking. "You sure?"

"Truly, Colt. I'm fine." My body is fine, but I doubt if my heart will ever recover.

"Thank goodness. I thought I might have to let you out of this bed, and I'm not ready to do that."

She smiled, loving him so much that she longed to lie here in his arms all day, but she'd heard Evan fussing and needed to check on him. "I'd better tend to the baby."

Reluctantly slipping from beneath the covers, she rummaged around in search of her robe and put it on.

"He's not crying." Colt stretched a hand toward her, a sexy quirk lifting his mouth. "Come back to bed."

Kati teetered indecisively, certain she'd heard the baby fussing. Colt's heavy-lidded gaze drew her. She went to the door, opened it and listened. Hearing nothing she closed it again.

"I told you he's okay," Colt murmured lazily. "I'm the one who's suffering."

"You, sir, are a glutton." Boldly she launched herself at him. He caught her in midair, stripped her giggling form of the robe and rubbed his whiskered cheek against her belly.

A long time passed before they got around to checking on Evan.

* * *

Weak-kneed and smiling, Kati made her way toward the baby's room. Last night and this morning had been like nothing else she'd ever experienced. Colt seemed so attentive, so playful, so…loving. A rosy aura of joy surrounded her.

What did it matter if he'd danced with other women? He'd come home with her. And had spent the night making her feel beautiful and desirable. He'd said they should enjoy each other while they could. So for now she wouldn't let herself think of their impending divorce.

Humming softly, she pushed open the door of the nursery. No doubt Evan was past ready for breakfast.

He lay on his back, arms flung wide to the sides, knees flopped outward. Kati bent toward him to lovingly stroke the dark hair. Ripples of terror shot through her. Evan's cheeks glowed red and his breathing came in harsh rasps. Scorching heat emanated from his body.

"Oh, my God."

Other than a summer cold, he'd never been sick. She lifted him from the crib, horrified when he vomited with violent force and began to shake. He opened glazed eyes and whimpered.

"Colt!" she shrieked, trembling so violently she had difficulty cleaning his face and divesting him of the ruined clothing. "Colt, hurry!"

Panic took over. She couldn't think what to do. She yanked the shivering baby against her breast and prayed.

After what seemed like forever, Colt rounded the doorway. "Don't tell me he's started walking—"

The words died in his throat as he took in the feverish child and Kati's anxious face. He placed a palm to the baby's head.

"Hell's bells, Kati, he's burning up. Have you taken his temperature?"

At her negative response, he grabbed the ear thermometer from the dresser and handed it to her.

As the reading appeared, Kati began to cry. "Oh, no."

"One hundred five degrees." Colt thrust the machine back in its place. "Get dressed. We've got to get him to a doctor."

Evan's high-pitched wail sent shards of terror and guilt jabbing through the adults. They exchanged frightened glances and shifted into high gear, running toward the bedroom for clothes.

In five minutes flat they were in the truck headed for town. Kati carried a bag of ice cubes and two wet washcloths which she used to bathe Evan's blazing body.

Halfway to town, he convulsed, his chubby body arching piteously as he struggled against some unknown illness.

The truck had already been flying over the highway, but now Colt coaxed the engine to a faster pace as Kati prayed aloud. She was helpless to do more.

At the hospital's emergency entrance, Kati barreled out of the door before the truck stopped rolling. With Evan in her arms, she ran into the building.

"Somebody, please," she screamed. "Help my baby!"

Two nurses came running. One took the baby from her shaking arms and disappeared into an exam room. Unwilling to let Evan out of her sight, Kati followed, her long hair flowing in tangled disarray around her shoulders. She knew how wild and unkempt she must look but didn't care. All that mattered now was Evan.

As she answered a barrage of questions, Colt appeared at her side and slipped an arm around her waist. She leaned into him, grateful for his strength, afraid that any moment she'd collapse in a babbling heap.

"Where's the doctor?" Colt sounded angry.

"On his way." A redheaded nurse whose nametag read Breanna Washburn glanced up from the table where she efficiently bathed Evan's heated body. "He was on the golf course."

"What the hell's he doing out there when this baby is so sick?" The tense muscles in Colt's arm tightened like steel bands against Kati's back.

"It's Sunday, sir." She came around the table and patted his arm. "Don't worry. He'll be here any minute."

The door swished open, and Dr. Connelson breezed in. "What have we got here?"

"High temp, convulsions, projectile vomiting." Nurse Washburn listed the symptoms.

After a quick initial exam, the doctor said, "Set up for a spinal tap. Call the pediatric floor and get him a bed, then make sure we have a tech in the lab who can get us a rapid read on this."

Nurse Washburn hurried away to follow his commands while the other nurse and Dr. Connelson tended to Evan.

"Mr. and Mrs. Garret," he said, "I think I know what's wrong with your baby, although we'll need to do a spinal tap to confirm. With your consent, we'll do that now, then get him started on an antibiotic IV and send him up to the pediatric unit."

"He'll have to stay in the hospital?" Kati's voice shook with terror. How had Evan come to be so sick so quickly?

"Undoubtedly," the doctor answered, then noted the

look of panic on Kati's face. "But you can stay with him."

"What's wrong with him?" Colt cut in.

"Looks like meningitis."

"Oh, dear God. Oh, Colt." Kati went limp with despair, crumbling against Colt's sturdy side. "Don't let him die. It'll be my fault if he dies."

"Hush, Kati." Colt wrapped her in a fierce embrace, pressing her face into his heaving chest. "It's no one's fault."

"Your husband's right, Mrs. Garret." Dr. Connelson talked as his experienced hands and eyes moved over Evan's limp body. "Meningitis is an infection that can follow a cold or ear infection. Sometimes it's caught from another infected child. There's no way you could have known or prevented it."

"He was fine last night." Fear edged Colt's voice.

"Meningitis happens that way sometimes. But he's in good hands, and from what you've told me, we've caught it early. The sooner we start treatment, the better chance he has of making a full recovery."

The words echoed in Kati's head like drumbeats. If she'd checked on Evan when she first awakened, she'd have discovered his illness hours ago. Guilt sliced through her like a stiletto. While she and Colt were romping in bed, Evan had been struggling for his life.

Colt paced the floor inside Evan's hospital room. In the three days and nights since they'd brought him in, neither he nor Kati had left the baby's side. Each time a nurse gently suggested that one of them go home and sleep, Colt had angrily brushed the idea aside.

How could he sleep when Evan might die? How could he go on living if Evan did die? Natosha Parker, for whatever reason, had entrusted the boy to his care, and he'd let them both down.

Kati sat in a chair beside Evan's crib, one hand inside the rails holding the IV in his arm. She'd been in that spot almost constantly since the beginning, blaming herself for Evan's illness. But Colt knew she wasn't to blame. The fault was his. Kati had wanted to check on the boy, but he had selfishly lured her back into the bed.

He slammed his eyes shut against the shame as his jesting words came back to haunt him. "I'm the one who's suffering," he'd said stupidly, foolishly, not knowing how wrong he was.

He scrubbed a hand over his unshaved face.

"Kati."

Red-rimmed eyes lifted to his. His gut twisted to see her this way. He wanted to go to her, hold her, comfort her, love her, but he didn't dare. Loving her had gotten them into this mess.

"Take the truck and go home, sweetheart. I promise I'll sit right there in that chair and hold his arm. I won't leave his side for a minute."

Her answer was filled with anguish. "I love him, Colt, as much as if he were really mine."

He knelt beside her, aching so that he thought his heart would burst. Kati—sweet, sweet Kati—was suffering, too, all because of his self-gratifying lust.

"I know you love him," he told her gently, stroking her cheek. "No birth mother could have taken any better care of him than you have."

"I didn't mean to fall in love with him," she rambled on, dry-eyed and haunted. "I was so worried about having to leave him, but now I'm afraid he's going to leave me."

"Shh. Stop that. Evan is going to make it. He's tough and strong, thanks to you. He'll beat this thing."

"I'm scared."

"So am I, baby." He pulled her against him, resting her head on his shoulder. "But the doctors say he's improving. His fever is down some, and he's not having those seizures anymore. He's gonna beat this thing."

"But what if his little brain is damaged? He's so smart, Colt." She clawed at his shoulders. "What if he's lost that?"

The doctors had warned them about the possible complication, and Colt was as riveted by fear as Kati, though he refused to acknowledge it.

As distraught as Kati was, discussing the possibility would only stress her more. She looked like a frightened, abandoned child, and Colt's gut wrenched to know she'd probably looked exactly the same during her days in foster care. He ached to comfort her, to take her home and make her world safe and happy again, to give her the security she'd never had and all the love inside him.

There was that word again—*love*. He turned the idea over in his head, remembering the Garret curse. He had no business thinking of Kati in terms of love. Not with his family history. Garrets inevitably ended up hurting those they professed to care about. He'd always known that, yet, true to form, he'd stepped over the line and let Kati and Evan get too close. And now they were suffering because of him.

Kati needed his strength and he'd give her that, but anything else would only cause her more pain down the road. And he'd already hurt her enough.

Very tenderly he kissed her on the cheek and went back to his place beside the window.

* * *

Two more days passed and still Colt and Kati remained at Evan's side, taking turns sitting next to him while one slept on a narrow cot near his crib. Even at that, they slept only briefly, popping up each time Evan stirred or when a nurse or doctor opened the door.

Kati lay on the cot, staring up at the ceiling, praying that God would let her die instead of allowing Evan to be brain damaged. Though Dr. Connelson had finally assured them that Evan would live, he couldn't promise that the baby would be himself again. Guilt gnawed away at her. Had the time she'd spent in bed with Colt stolen Evan's intellect?

Weary and aching with regret, she raised herself up, swinging her legs over the side. Though Jett and Cookie had come daily with changes of clothes for both her and Colt, Kati felt grungy. The quick sponge baths in the tiny bathroom had been all she'd allow herself.

At her movement, Colt glanced her way. "You didn't sleep very long."

"Let me go to the bathroom, and I'll take over so you can rest awhile."

He'd opened his mouth to protest when the loveliest sound either of them had heard in days came from the crib.

"Da-da-da-da-da-da."

Kati catapulted across the room. Colt stretched a hand inside the rails where he was met by a pudgy hand slapping playfully at his. A wide, pink-gummed smile greeted the two dumbfounded adults.

"He's better," Kati whispered around the lump in her throat.

"He knows us, Kati." Colt's voice was filled with wonder. "Look at him. He knows us."

Evan's eyes were alive with intelligence. Babbling, he stretched two chubby arms upward. Relief, pure and precious, filled the room.

Taking care not to disturb his IV, Colt hoisted Evan into his arms and turned toward Kati.

"Come here, sweetheart," he said gruffly. "I need to hold you both."

With a grateful sob, Kati walked into his arms, the baby they loved between them.

Chapter Eleven

In the weeks following Evan's illness, Kati barely let him out of her sight. Though the child recovered quickly and completely, no antibiotic existed for Kati's guilt.

She had been hired to care for Evan, and she'd failed him. That Colt held her responsible, too, was obvious, regardless of his words to the contrary. He'd proved as much on the day they brought Evan home from the hospital when he'd moved his belongings out of Kati's room without so much as a word. Since then, he hadn't touched her. He remained friendly and charming, taking his meals with her, sharing time with Evan, but there was no return to their former closeness. She was the nanny and nothing more. Funny how the marriage of convenience she'd asked for seemed so unsatisfactory now.

Though the thought depressed her, Kati knew the break was inevitable. The small apartment she'd had built on one side of the day-care center was nearly complete. Their time together was almost over.

"You going in to that center of yours again today?" Cookie cracked two eggs into a bowl, beating each in turn with a wire whisk.

Kati had come into the kitchen for Evan's bottles. She took them from the refrigerator and slipped them into the diaper bag.

"I'll be back in time for supper."

"Don't seem like you're ever here no more," he complained, dumping two cups of sugar into the eggs and beating the combination with enough energy to mix concrete.

"Cookie," Kati said gently, "the center is almost ready to open. Another week and I'll be gone for good."

Leaving the blustery old man with sprouts for hair would be almost as hard as leaving Colt and Evan. He'd become as much a part of her temporary family as they had.

"Ain't right," he grumbled. "You two was made for each other. I don't know what's got into you."

What had gotten into them was guilt. That, and the realization that they were playing a game no one could win. Kati's fantasy of a real family and Colt's desire for bachelorhood were not exactly compatible. It had taken Evan's illness to wake them both up.

The dream catcher Colt had bought her hung above the bed. She knew the device must work because all her bad dreams came in the daylight. Nighttime brought dreams of Colt holding her, loving her, chanting her name in a way that made her feel so cherished and beautiful. Kati still awakened every morning expecting to see Colt's mischievous grin or feel his powerful body next to hers. Waking was the hardest part of the day.

"How's that center of yours look?"

Cookie's question drew her back to the kitchen. She tried to muster enthusiasm in her answer. After all, Kati's Angels was her dream, the only one likely to ever come true.

"The center looks fantastic, Cookie. You should come with me sometime and check it out." She sneaked a spoon of cookie dough from the bowl and received a mock scowl in return. "I'm going to miss your cooking. Maybe I can even lure you away from the Garrets and have you cook for me."

"Me? In a room full of little tots? Ain't likely, Miss Kati. Evan's the only little 'un I've ever been around. But I will make some cookies for you once in a while. These yahoos around here don't appreciate nothing."

"I'll remember that."

"You remember this, too, missy." He waved a spatula in her direction. "That road out there runs both ways. I expect a visit now and then."

Rising on tiptoe, Kati planted a kiss on the old man's cheek. He blustered and stuttered before returning to his cookie dough.

"See you later, Cookie."

After checking the diaper bag for supplies, Kati headed to the nursery for Evan. He was into everything now, and the only way she could get things done was to put him in the playpen for brief periods.

Seeing Kati, the boy pulled himself upright and threw a stuffed bear over the side. Kati retrieved the toy and handed it back, only to have the thing come flying at her again. Playing fetch with Kati was his newest game.

"You little rascal." She scooped him up for kisses and giggles.

While she stored the sound of his delighted laughter, a different voice broke in.

"Kati."

Colt appeared in the doorway. The time was mid-morning, an unusual hour for him to come to the house. His warm, sweaty scent stirred memories of better times between them. He looked ill-at-ease, tense, swallowing twice before he spoke again.

"I need to talk to you. Will you bring Evan into my office, please?"

So polite. So serious. Kati knew something was wrong. Butterflies stirred in her belly. Was he going to replace her as Evan's nanny? The blade of guilt sliced her. She knew she deserved to be fired after what she'd done.

Anxiously she carried the baby to Colt's study.

"Sit down, please."

There was the courtesy again, the softening of the inevitable blow.

"What's wrong, Colt?" She eased into a chair, letting Evan wiggle down onto the carpet. "You're making me very nervous."

"There's no easy way to say this."

She gripped the chair arm. "If you're firing me, just say it. But I beg you to let me go on keeping Evan. I love him. I'll take good care of him from now on. Please, Colt, let him come to the center with me when I go."

Colt shook his head and frowned, his expression puzzled. "Jace Bristow drove out this morning to bring some news."

"Your attorney?"

Colt took a deep breath, sighing deeply. "The private investigator found Natosha Parker."

The air around Kati buzzed so loudly she couldn't think. Evan's mother had been found.

A sharp, searing pain cut through her heart. She'd expected to lose Colt, but to lose Evan, too, after the horrific battle to save his life was more than she could bear.

What an idiot she'd been to let herself love these two males so much. She should have been prepared for this. Had even told herself that she could handle the inevitable separation. Hadn't a life in foster homes taught her that nothing lasted forever? But none of that mattered one whit in the face of losing her baby boy.

She didn't see Colt move, but suddenly he was kneeling beside her, holding her hand. She felt icy against the heat of his skin.

"Kati, I'm sorry. We both knew there was a chance Evan's mother would be found."

Through stiff lips she asked, "When will she come for him?"

Evan crawled to Colt's side and pulled up, gripping the cowboy's upraised knee. Colt's gaze flickered to the boy, then back to Kati's face.

"I don't know for sure. Jace says the P.I. tracked her to Europe, though he hasn't actually talked to her. He'll call us when he has more information."

"Europe." Kati squeezed her eyes closed against the pain. "Evan's mother went to Europe? And left her baby with strangers?"

Colt's mouth formed a grim line. "Looks that way."

Kati envisioned a female version of Evan gaily flitting around Europe, picnicking beneath the Eiffel Tower, sunning on the Riviera, while her child struggled for life in a remote Texas hospital. What kind of woman would do such a thing?

Only a woman who didn't really want her child.

Hope rekindled. "Maybe she won't want him back."

Natosha Parker didn't even know her son. She hadn't seen him in nearly six months. She hadn't walked the floor with him when he had colic. She hadn't stood beside his crib while he battled meningitis. Why, she didn't even know how much he loved Cookie's banana pudding. What right did she have to come waltzing back to town and reclaim Evan as her own?

"We could fight her for him." Kati clutched Colt's arm as the idea took hold. "You have the money to do it, and Jace is a good attorney."

Before she could finish, Colt shook his head. "No."

He pulled away and stood, turning his back. "Courts always side with birth mothers. If she wants him, he belongs with her."

Kati slumped in defeat. Colt had never wanted Evan, any more than he'd wanted a wife. Why had she thought he'd fight to keep him?

Evan would be gone, really gone. Natosha Parker would take him off to Europe, and Kati would never see him again.

This was the kind of thing that always happened when she allowed herself to love. She'd be leaving Garret Ranch with a twice-broken heart. The two people she'd fallen in love with would be as far away as the moon.

Somewhere life had taken a turn, spinning out of control. Her head pounded with the stress of it. She wanted the agony to stop. She wanted this entire charade to end before she shattered into a million little pieces at Colt's feet.

The time had come to let go. The pain couldn't possibly get any worse, so she might as well make the break now. Kati sat up straighter in the chair and took a deep breath. When she spoke, the words sounded surprisingly normal.

"So. When are you going to the Dominican Republic to arrange the divorce?"

Kati's question ricocheted off Colt like rifle shots off a rock wall. Staring down at Kati with her pale face and wide, haunted eyes, he tried to read what was behind the unexpected question. He knew their time was up. With Evan on the verge of reuniting with his mother, there was no point in prolonging the agony, but somehow he hadn't expected the moment to hurt so much or happen so soon.

"Kati's Angels will be finished in a week or so." Her hands gripped the chair arms with such ferocity that her knuckles were white. "I'd like to have the divorce final before I move out."

So that's how she wanted it. A clean break, a don't-look-back kind of parting. He should have known that's how she'd handle it. After all, she had what she came for—a business of her own.

Bitterness crept into his consciousness. Kati had used him, a fact that shouldn't have bothered him. She'd admitted from the start to only needing a husband as collateral for her loan. And he'd used her, too, selfishly worming his way into her bed, when he'd known all along he had nothing else to offer. He glanced at the baby happily banging a set of plastic keys against the carpet—Evan had paid dearly for that.

Colt stalked to the window, hands thrust in his back pockets, and leaned his forehead against the pane. She was right; he knew she was right. Every night when he crawled into his bed alone, he fought the temptation to go to her. He wanted her so much he couldn't sleep for thinking of her soft skin, her clean scent, her glorious hair tangled around him. But he couldn't give in to lust again. He'd already hurt them all enough. Kati was right. A divorce was the only way to be rid of the temptation…and the guilt.

"I'll call the airline today." He returned to his desk and jotted a reminder, as if he'd need one. Getting a divorce wasn't likely to slip his mind.

"How long do you think it will take?"

He glanced up, noting again how pale she looked. "The divorce?"

She nodded, and her long loose hair fell forward, distracting him. He wanted desperately to go to her and bury his hands in the flowing strands, to kiss her until she uttered those soft, kitten sounds that made him feel so big and tough and strong. But Kati didn't want that. She wanted her day-care center and a divorce. He'd given her the first, and now he'd have to give her the second, even if it killed him.

"One day over and one day back according to Jace." He swallowed thickly. "It's the easiest place in the world to get a divorce."

"One day over," she said vaguely. "One day."

Evan pulled up next to her, banging away with his keys. With the natural ease of a mother, Kati lifted him onto her lap and kissed the top of his head.

Emotion tugged at Colt's heart. No woman, not even Natosha Parker, could love that baby more than Kati. She was his mother, in every way except the one that counted most. He wished he could change that for her.

To give her Evan. To give her... He shook his head in irritation. Hell, he couldn't give her anything.

"Will you be all right?" he asked.

She smiled a trifle too brightly. "I'll be fine. As soon as my center opens I'll be too busy with all those babies to even think straight."

"It's what you wanted, then?"

"I've dreamed about that business for years." The smile still in place, Kati stood, bringing Evan with her. "In fact, I was on my way into town to take care of some details when you arrived."

Colt watched her walk the length of the room and disappear out the door, her long, swaying hair a reminder of all he was losing.

Slumping into a chair, he dropped his head into his hands.

Soon he'd be rid of her. His life would return to normal. No more baby toys to stumble over. No more perfume clouding the fresh country air. He should be happy, overjoyed, exuberant.

Then why did he feel as if he'd been gored by a bull?

The silver BMW blended with the damp, gray October day as it wheeled beneath the Garret Ranch sign and sped toward the house. From her vantage point in the living room, Kati saw the vehicle coming and went to the door.

A nice-looking man about Colt's age emerged from the car and strolled toward her. Though smaller than Colt, he was fit and trim and exuded an almost palpable energy.

"You must be Kati. I'm Jace," he said without fanfare, and strode into the ranch house as though he needed no invitation to enter. He swiped his boots across the rug Cookie had spread in front of the door. "Where's Colt?"

"At the barn."

"On a rotten day like this? I thought he'd be home."

"One of his best mares foaled last night. If you know Colt, you know he has to check on that foal every few hours." She led the way into the living room and motioned for him to sit. "He'll be back soon. Would you like some coffee while you wait?"

"Why not? One more cup won't kill me." The lawyer perched on the edge of a straight-back chair. "They say lawyers bleed money, but in actuality, we bleed coffee."

He hopped up and marched restlessly to the window, looking out, while Kati went after the coffee.

Just as she returned, the door flew open and Colt stomped into the room, droplets of rain dripping from his hat.

"Nasty day." He tossed the Stetson toward the coffee table.

"You're getting the floor wet," Kati admonished mildly.

Colt lifted one boot, then the other.

"Sorry." He backtracked to the door and wiped his feet on the mat.

Jace cast a curious look between the two, then turned his attention to Evan, who sat in front of the entertainment center, busily emptying every VCR tape from its shelves.

"This must be Evan." He settled once more into a chair, looking ready to spring up at any moment. Kati thought of the jack-in-the-box in Evan's room.

"What's up, Jace?" Colt wiped a damp sleeve over

his face. "You didn't drive all this way in the pouring rain for coffee."

"Right." Jace tossed a file folder on the table. "I have more news of Natosha Parker."

Colt stilled, his gaze traveling from Kati to the baby. "When is she coming for him?"

"She isn't." The lawyer paused dramatically, and Kati envisioned him standing before a jury in a murder trial. The air was electric with his unspoken news.

"Why?" Colt asked, frowning. "Doesn't she want him back?"

"Natosha Parker is dead."

The horrible words pulsated in the room as their meaning found its way into Kati's consciousness.

"Oh." She slithered into a chair, hand at her throat. "Poor Evan. Poor, motherless Evan."

Colt moved to her side and laid a hand on her shoulder. Just that small gesture buoyed her sagging strength.

"What happened to her?"

Jace gazed from Colt's hand to Kati's stricken face. "Cancer. She went to Europe for one of those experimental drugs that aren't available here in the states. According to their records, she died within three weeks of her arrival."

"So that's why she dumped Evan on my doorstep and disappeared. She knew she was dying and wanted to leave him in a safe place." Colt accepted the file from Jace and flipped through it. "But why me? I don't even know who she was."

"The P.I. faxed some info he picked up in Europe." Jace took the folder and extracted a sheet of paper. "It's not much and from the handwriting she was very weak, but she left this with a nurse. Problem was, she lapsed into a coma before telling anyone where to send it. She thanks you again and apologizes for sending a letter of explanation with the baby instead of coming herself. Says she couldn't take the chance that you might refuse. And under the circumstances she knew you'd understand." Jace glanced up from the document. "You never mentioned a letter."

Colt looked from Jace to the baby, bewildered. "That's because there wasn't one."

A letter would have made things so much simpler for Colt. And impossible for Kati. "What could have happened to it?"

"We'll probably never know now, but it obviously was lost somewhere along the way. There is a picture in here, though." Jace withdrew a photo which he handed to Colt. "Maybe this will ring a bell."

"Tassie!" Colt said, flipping his knuckles at the picture. "That's Tassie."

"So you do know her."

"Yeah. Well, sort of, though I didn't know her name was Natosha. We called her Tassie. Shoot, I'd even forgotten her last name." He scooted Kati's hand from the chair arm and perched there beside her, earning another odd glance from his attorney. "Two, maybe three years ago, she came out with the college kids. You know." He glanced at Jace. "The internship thing we do every summer. They come for a couple of months, work with the hands, and then they're gone. I'm usually too busy to remember much about them." He handed the photo to Kati. "That year was kind of different because two of them were girls interested in cutting horses. Since that's my specialty, the girls spent more time with me than usual."

"Natosha was one of those girls?"

"Yeah."

"The two of you must have formed some kind of bond."

"She was a nice kid, kind of quiet, who had a way with horses."

"You obviously made an impression on her."

All three of them glanced at the baby.

"Come to think of it she did say I reminded her of her dad a few times." Colt grimaced. "Made me feel like an old man. But she obviously thought a lot of her folks. Wonder why she didn't leave Evan with them."

"She couldn't. Her parents were all the family she had, and they were killed by a drunk driver about a year before Evan was born. The insurance money paid for her trip to Europe."

"Poor kid." Colt shook his head. "What about Evan's father?"

"There's not one listed on the birth certificate."

"Oh, Colt." Kati squeezed Colt's thigh as she stared at the very young face of Natosha Parker, the mother Evan would never know. Pity and sorrow welled up in her. "I had such ugly thoughts about her, and all the time she was only trying to do what was best for her baby."

"Yeah." He stroked her hand, soothingly, obliviously, as he spoke to Jace. "So where do we go from here?"

"The next move is yours." Jace slipped the papers back into the folder, leaving the file on the table. "Evan is highly adoptable at this point in his life. I have a number of clients who would take him tomorrow if you choose not to keep him."

"This has all happened too fast for me. I'll have to think on it."

"You do that. There's no hurry. Wait until you return

from the Caribbean if you like.'' He paused and studied Colt and Kati who sat on the same chair, holding hands. ''You are still getting a divorce, aren't you?''

''Yeah.'' With a puzzled expression, Colt looked at Kati's hand in his, released his hold and rose to accompany Jace to the door. ''I'm flying out tomorrow.''

Kati watched the two men move into the foyer, their conversation carrying back to her.

''The two of you sure seem friendly,'' she heard Jace remark. ''Are you certain a divorce is the right thing?''

A long silence ensued before Colt replied. ''I'm not the marrying kind, Jace. You know my background. Everybody in my family is divorced or miserable in marriage. We'll both be better off when this thing is over and done.''

Another long silence followed. Then Jace said the strangest thing. ''Sounds to me like you've got some heavy thinking to do, boy. Call me when you make up your mind…about both of them.''

Chapter Twelve

Cranky as a stud horse in a pasture of cows, Colt settled into the window seat and stretched his long legs forward as far as possible. Hell's bells, why couldn't they make these blasted airplanes big enough for a man to be comfortable? And where the hell was that flight attendant with the drinks? If he had to be squeezed in like a calf in a head gate, the least they could do was bring him some booze.

He yanked at his tie, loosened it and wondered why the hell he'd worn the thing in the first place. He hated ties. He hated airplanes. And he hated the awful ache in his gut every time he thought of what this trip meant.

"Excuse me." A voice interrupted his furious musings. "Is this seat twelve B?"

Great. Just what he didn't need—company.

"Yes, ma'am."

She indicated her carry-on. "Would you mind?"

He removed his hat, stifling a sigh. "No problem."

Politely, just as his mama had taught him, he helped

the tiny, silver-haired woman stash her bag in the overhead space, squeezed his knees a little closer to his body and resigned himself to a seat mate for the flight to the Dominican Republic. Hopefully she wasn't a talker.

"The plane is fuller than usual today, isn't it?"

"I don't fly that often, ma'am. I wouldn't know."

"Oh, my. I make the trip at least once a month."

Despite his reluctance to talk, he arched an eyebrow and said, "Every month?"

She didn't look like the fun-in-the-sun Caribbean type.

The little woman laughed. "My grandbabies live there. Their mama married one of those baseball players." She fumbled for her purse, a black rectangular thing with a gold clasp on the top. "Let me show you their pictures. They're the prettiest kids you've ever seen."

Colt wanted to slap her little spotted hands and tell her to leave the photos where they were. Respect for his elders kept him still.

"This is Matthew." She thrust a "Grandma's brag book" beneath his nose. "He's six. You should hear that boy read. Why, I know for a fact he's the smartest child in his class."

A gap-toothed boy as freckled as an Appaloosa horse grinned out at Colt. He smiled in spite of his bad mood.

"Cute kid."

"This is baby Wade." She tapped a finger at a blue-eyed child about Evan's age. "My daughter lost a little girl in between the boys, so when Wade came along, he was all the more special."

Touched, Colt shook his head. "I can understand that. When Evan had meningitis, it was the worst time of my life."

"Is Evan your son?"

"He's…" Rather than share his complicated story with a stranger, Colt grappled for his wallet. "Would you like to see his picture?"

"Of course."

He produced the only photo he had—Kati and him triumphantly holding the most beautiful baby in Rattlesnake, Texas.

"What a lovely family."

"Yeah." His focus swiveled from Kati's delighted smile to Evan's pudgy, waving fingers. "They're pretty special."

"So the baby's fully recovered from his illness."

"We were worried that he might suffer brain damage, but with Kati taking care of him, he recovered real fast." He shook his head and smiled. "Kati. She's something."

"It's plain to see you love your family, and that's a blessed thing these days." The woman patted his arm. "Too many men don't have enough sense to appreciate what they've got."

Remembering his destination, Colt clapped the wallet shut. "Some people aren't cut out for marriage, I guess."

"My late husband had a crazy notion like that. He thought he'd make a terrible husband because his daddy was. I thought I would never convince him that he didn't have to make the same mistakes as his father."

The woman went right on talking, but Colt didn't hear another word. Her story hit him right square in the gut. Just like her husband, he'd been convinced that he could never be marriage material, but for the past six months he'd done a pretty darn good job of it. He hadn't been perfect, but if Kati was really his, forever, he'd work his tail off to make her happy. His family's mistakes didn't have to be his.

As if his blinded eyes could suddenly see, he reopened the wallet and stared down at Kati and Evan. His family. His loves.

What was he doing on this blasted airplane?

Kati's Angels looked wonderful. The centers were set up, just begging for children to play in them. Murals of fairy-tale characters covered the walls, and gleaming, new, coat cubbies waited to be filled. The infant section glowed with brightly colored cribs and changing tables, toys and puzzles.

Though the grand opening wasn't until next week, Kati already had applications for over two-thirds of the available places. She'd hired two helpers and hoped to add two more by opening day. Everything about the center was just as she'd always dreamed.

She hung up the phone and rubbed the knot forming in the back of her neck. The center was perfect, but her life was a shambles.

Up until the time Colt left for the airport this morning, she'd held out a tiny seed of hope that they might work something out. He had to know she loved him. But love from a woman like her wasn't enough to hold a man like Colt.

Evan, trying to cut a tooth, had fussed relentlessly all morning. She wanted nothing more than to take him home to his own room and put him to bed. The thought brought a derisive smile. Like her, Evan didn't really have a home, or a bed, of his own. They were both living on the good graces of someone who no longer wanted either of them.

With a heavy sigh she decided to go back to the ranch and start packing. Wallowing in self-pity had never gained her a thing.

The old tomcat protested the mess Kati made in the bedroom. Every time she started to put a stack of clothes or books into a box, Caesar lay inside, curled in a ball.

"Get out of there, you old reprobate."

He stretched and yawned, then stalked haughtily to the next empty carton.

Kati shook her head and finished packing. All she had left to do was change the sheets and clean the bathroom, so Cookie wouldn't have to do it.

She'd put the finishing touches on the bed and bent to straighten the dust ruffle when something white caught her eye. From behind the headboard, she extracted one of Colt's T-shirts.

Holding the garment in both hands, she plopped down on the bed, remembering all the times he'd ripped his shirt off in front of her and teased her when she'd blushed. Slowly, deliberately, she raised the garment to her face, inhaling the scent that belonged only to the man she loved. She hadn't meant to love him. Hadn't wanted to open herself up to that kind of heartache. But she had. And even though the pain of losing him ripped at her like sharks' teeth, never to have loved him at all would be even worse. Loving Colt Garret had been a risk worth taking.

The dam inside her burst. She, who thought she had no tears left, began to sob.

"Oh, Colt," she moaned, holding his shirt close to her trembling body. "I love you. I love you."

The cat leaped upon the bed, rubbing his sleek form

against her arms. But Kati knew no comfort and continued to cry softly, her heart breaking.

In the far reaches of her mind she heard a door open and close, and struggled to regain her composure. For Cookie to catch her crying like a wounded child wouldn't do. She blotted her face with Colt's shirt, but a fresh wave of grief surfaced as his scent rose from the garment.

"Kati."

Her head snapped up at the deep voice.

"Colt!" Slapping at her tears, Kati poked the shirt behind her. "You're back already?"

"Uh-huh." Dressed in his Western-cut jacket and blue jeans, he stood in the doorway taking in her disheveled appearance and the packing boxes stacked in one corner. He held a sheaf of papers in one hand. "What are you doing?"

He came toward her, hovered momentarily, then settled on the bed beside her, his thigh brushing hers. He was uncomfortably close, dangerously close. Tears threatened to resurface. She'd wanted to be gone when he returned.

"Packing. I thought it would be better this way." She swallowed the knot in her throat and asked the ugly question. "Did you get the divorce?"

Colt sat silently for a long moment, and when he spoke he didn't say what she'd expected. In a low, throaty voice filled with painful intensity, he asked, "Do you love me?"

Shock waves pulsated through Kati. She couldn't have answered even if she'd known what to say.

He touched her then—just his fingertips lightly placed atop her hand, but the gentle contact shook her to the core.

"Cookie says you do," he continued in that intense voice. "Jett says you do. I have to know the truth." He pivoted toward her, expression tormented. "Do you?"

Kati choked back a fresh wave of despair. Why was he doing this? He wasn't a cruel man. Why would he ask such a thing when he held divorce papers in his hands? Bereft, she stared down at her lap where somehow the cotton shirt had reappeared.

"Tell me, Kati." Colt gripped her chin and forced her gaze to his. "I have to know. Please."

Dark brown eyes pierced her, tearing the words from her very soul. She could no more hide the truth than she could rise and fly.

"With all my heart," she whispered, unshed tears pressing at the back of her throat. "With all my soul."

"Oh, Kati," he groaned, crushing her to him in a breath-stopping embrace. "We almost made a terrible mistake."

Kati's head reeled. Her heart pounded. What was he saying?

Suddenly he pushed away and fumbled in his jacket pocket. Then he slid to the floor, resting on one knee.

"Kati." He opened the velvet box to display a sparkling diamond ring. "Will you be my wife, my real wife, forever?"

"I don't understand."

"Do you love me or not?" he asked in exasperation.

"Yes."

"And I love you. I've been in love with you since the very first, and I was too mule-headed to see the truth. My family is so filled with divorces I had this notion that I'd have to get one, too. It took nearly losing you to bring me to my senses."

Wondrously, Kati watched him slide the ring onto her finger. "But how? What changed your mind?"

"Everyone could see the truth except me. Cookie, Jett, Jace, even a white-haired grandma on the plane." He wagged his head. "This morning before I left, Cookie read me the riot act, threatened to quit or poison me or both if I didn't wake up and see that this crazy marriage of ours was the real thing. I told him you only wanted that day care, not me, and he threw an egg at me, calling me a confounded, blind cowpuncher without a lick of sense."

Kati smiled. "I love that man."

"Me, too." He gave her a lopsided grin. "All the way to the Dominican, I thought about what he said. Then that little grandma on the plane told me how lucky I was to have you. By the time the plane landed, I missed you and Evan so much I hopped the next flight home. I want to make this marriage work, the real deal, no holding back. Do you think we can?"

"I'm willing to try if you are."

"No. I won't try."

Her heart plummeted. "But I thought you just said—"

"Shh." He cupped her cheek. "I don't want to *try*, Kati. I want to *succeed*. Forget our wretched family histories. I want to spend the rest of my life with the woman I love and that little boy in there."

Caesar rose from his spot on Kati's pillow to insinuate himself between the couple. He pressed suggestively against Colt's chest.

"And my cat?" Kati asked in amusement.

"I hate cats." But he stroked the sleek gray fur just the same.

Kati took his hand and returned it to her cheek. "Don't make me jealous of my own cat."

"Our cat," he countered with a wink.

Laughing softly, she snuggled into his arms, scarcely able to believe that her fantasy had come to life. "I thought you blamed me for Evan's illness."

"No, darlin', I blamed myself, not you. But today I realized the doctor was right. No one could have prevented what happened. Our loving each other was a gift and we shouldn't ever doubt that again. We never neglected Evan. We've been good parents." He kissed her on the forehead, then pulled back and said, "Which reminds me. I have another present." He reached for the sheaf of papers that had fallen to the floor.

Puzzled, she took the legal-looking documents. "What is this?"

"I stopped by Jace's office on the way home. All you have to do is sign them, and you and I will be mama and daddy to Evan forever."

"Oh, Colt, I love you." She couldn't seem to say the words enough.

"I love you, too, Mrs. Garret." He took the papers from her and dropped them onto the bed. Standing, he swept Kati into his arms and started down the hall, kissing her all the way.

"Where are we going?" she whispered against his lips.

"Where we should have been on our wedding night."

He kicked open the door to the master bedroom and carried her inside. Laying her on the king-size bed, he followed her down, his hands and mouth burning trails of longing over her skin.

"I will love you forever, Kati Garret," he murmured

against her ear, his hands expertly removing the clip from her braid. "Will you always love me, too?"

"Forever and ever," she whispered, heart soaring.

With slow, sensual strokes, Colt ran his fingers through her hair, watching it fall around her shoulders, adoring her with his eyes and lips and hands.

As he worked his tender magic, pressing her deeper and deeper into the bed they would share as husband and wife, Kati knew joy as sweet and pure as Evan's laughter. She, Kati Winslow Garret, after a lifetime of temporary houses and temporary families, had finally and forever come home.

*   *   *   *   *

Look for Linda Goodnight's
HER PREGNANT AGENDA
in October 2003,
part of Silhouette Romance's
engaging continuity
MARRYING THE BOSS'S DAUGHTER

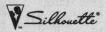
Silhouette®

INTIMATE MOMENTS™

From *New York Times* bestselling author

SUZANNE BROCKMANN

Night Watch
(Silhouette Intimate Moments #1243)

Navy SEAL Wes Skelly has come to Hollywood to act as a
bodyguard for a beautiful young TV star. Then a blind date
leads to romance after Wes meets Brittany Evans. But soon
ideas of happily-ever-after come crashing down as the stalker
who was the motivation for Wes's Hollywood move finds a
new target—in Brittany.

A brand-new *Tall, Dark & Dangerous* book!

Available September 2003 at your favorite retail outlet.

If you enjoyed what you just read,
then we've got an offer you can't resist!

Take 2 bestselling love stories FREE!

Plus get a FREE surprise gift!

Clip this page and mail it to Silhouette Reader Service™

IN U.S.A.	**IN CANADA**
3010 Walden Ave.	P.O. Box 609
P.O. Box 1867	Fort Erie, Ontario
Buffalo, N.Y. 14240-1867	L2A 5X3

YES! Please send me 2 free Silhouette Romance® novels and my free surprise gift. After receiving them, if I don't wish to receive anymore, I can return the shipping statement marked cancel. If I don't cancel, I will receive 6 brand-new novels every month, before they're available in stores! In the U.S.A., bill me at the bargain price of $3.34 plus 25¢ shipping and handling per book and applicable sales tax, if any*. In Canada, bill me at the bargain price of $3.80 plus 25¢ shipping and handling per book and applicable taxes**. That's the complete price and a savings of at least 10% off the cover prices—what a great deal! I understand that accepting the 2 free books and gift places me under no obligation ever to buy any books. I can always return a shipment and cancel at any time. Even if I never buy another book from Silhouette, the 2 free books and gift are mine to keep forever.

215 SDN DNUM
315 SDN DNUN

Name	(PLEASE PRINT)	
Address	Apt.#	
City	State/Prov.	Zip/Postal Code

* Terms and prices subject to change without notice. Sales tax applicable in N.Y.
** Canadian residents will be charged applicable provincial taxes and GST.
All orders subject to approval. Offer limited to one per household and not valid to current Silhouette Romance® subscribers.
® are registered trademarks of Harlequin Books S.A., used under license.

SROM02   ©1998 Harlequin Enterprises Limited

It's romantic comedy with a kick
(in a pair of strappy pink heels)!

Introducing

HARLEQUIN®

flipside™

"It's chick-lit with the romance and happily-ever-after ending that Harlequin is known for."
—*USA TODAY* bestselling author Millie Criswell, author of *Staying Single*, October 2003

"Even though our heroine may take a few false steps while finding her way, she does it with wit and humor."
—Dorien Kelly, author of *Do-Over*, November 2003

Launching October 2003.
Make sure you pick one up!

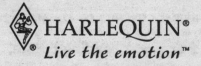

HARLEQUIN®
Live the emotion™

Visit us at www.harlequinflipside.com

HFGENERIC

SILHOUETTE *Romance*

COMING NEXT MONTH